PEA'S BOOK OF
BIRTHDAYS

Books by Susie Day

SUSIE DAY

PEA'S BOOK OF BIRTHDAYS

PUFFIN

PUFFIN BOOKS

UK | USA | Canada | Ireland | Australia
India | New Zealand | South Africa

Puffin Books is part of the Penguin Random House group of companies
whose addresses can be found at global.penguinrandomhouse.com.

www.penguin.co.uk
www.puffin.co.uk
www.ladybird.co.uk

First published in Great Britain by Red Fox,
an imprint of Random House Children's Publishers, 2013
This edition published by Puffin Books 2016

001

Typeset in 13.26/18.40 pt Baskerville MT by Falcon Oast Graphic Art
Printed in Great Britain by Clays Ltd, St Ives plc

A CIP catalogue record for this book is available from the British Library

ISBN: 978–0–141–37529–8

All correspondence to:
Puffin Books,
Penguin Random House Children's,
80 Strand, London WC2R 0RL

www.greenpenguin.co.uk

MIX
Paper from
responsible sources
FSC
www.fsc.org FSC® C018179

Penguin Random House is committed to a
sustainable future for our business, our readers
and our planet. This book is made from Forest
Stewardship Council® certified paper.

For Jess

CHAPTER 1

CLOVER IN WONDERLAND

It was the first of May, a Sunday, and behind the Llewellyn family's raspberry-red front door a birthday party was being prepared.

The house was in chaos.

Mum was frantically gluing playing cards onto string, like bunting.

Pea was icing the words EAT ME onto fairy cakes.

Tinkerbell was eating them.

Wuffly the dog was running around the garden, chewing an inflatable flamingo.

And Clover – whose birthday party it was – was locked in her bedroom, sulking.

Officially, Clover wouldn't turn fourteen until the following Thursday, but no one wants a birthday party on a Thursday. Unfortunately for her, this meant there was a pile of presents sitting in the front room, wrapped up and temptingly rattly, with a fierce Post-it note in Mum's handwriting stuck on top.

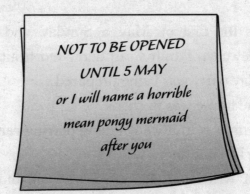

NOT TO BE OPENED
UNTIL 5 MAY
or I will name a horrible
mean pongy mermaid
after you

This was no idle threat. Mum was plain lovely Mum to the sisters – but to the rest of the world she was Marina Cove, the author of the bestselling

Mermaid Girls books. The fearsome Dreaditor had lately sent over her editorial notes on book five in the series. It was crammed with pirates and sea monsters (Pea had been allowed to read it before anyone else, and thought it might be the best yet) – and there was plenty of time for her to add a pongy Clover before it was printed for the world to see.

'I don't know why she's so moany when she's having two whole birthdays instead of one,' said Tinkerbell, licking yellow icing off her finger.

'Can't you get her to come down?' pleaded Mum. 'We've got all the cups to put out for the tea party yet, and all those sandwiches to cut up in triangles – and look, I've got jam in my hair . . . No, I don't know how either, but— Oh, Wuffly, don't eat that!' She disappeared into the garden.

Pea and Tinkerbell went upstairs, and knocked on Clover's bedroom door.

There was a pause. Then a note was pushed

under the door, in Clover's familiar curly hand-writing. It said:

I hate you all

'Rude,' said Tinkerbell, sticking out her bottom lip.

Before Pea could think of a suitable reply, another piece of paper shot out. This one said:

Go away !!!

It was swiftly followed by a third, with extra-curly letters and a drawing of a flower.

Please ❀

'Don't be fooled. She's only being polite to trick us into being nice to her,' whispered Tinkerbell. 'Never fear, the Amazing Tinkerbell is here to save the day!'

Stepping back, she plucked a red-and-purple magic wand from the waistband of her jeans, and brandished it at the door handle. '*Openus doorus!*' she yelled.

The door stayed shut.

'*Handleturn unlockleclock!*'

Again, the door stayed shut.

Tinkerbell tried shouting '*Dooranicum openify!*' too, but all that did was make the red-and-purple magic wand (which was actually two felt pens sellotaped together) sag in the middle, until the red end fell off.

'Oh, bottoms,' she muttered.

Pea sighed. Tinkerbell had become entirely magic-obsessed, ever since the Amazing Sylvester had made a dove appear between her hands at her friend Angelo's eighth birthday party last month. So far the Amazing Tinkerbell's magical repertoire ran to making chocolates vanish into her mouth and nothing else – but she had promised to make an egg pop out of Pea's ear very soon, whether Pea wanted one to or not.

'Perhaps magic isn't the best way to get her to open the door,' Pea suggested gently, taking the broken wand away.

Tinkerbell shrugged. 'Maybe. Oi, Clover!' she shouted, rapping hard on the door. 'Mum says I can eat all your birthday cake if you don't come out!'

'Tink!' hissed Pea. 'That's not what I meant!' She cleared her throat and knocked again, more softly. 'Clover? It's Pea. Mum didn't really say that about the cake. You know she wouldn't. Only it's after three o'clock already, and everyone's coming to your party at half past, so, um . . .'

There was a scratchy sound, followed by another note:

Tell my party guests I love them

A series of heartfelt sniffs emanated from behind the door. Pea and Tinkerbell exchanged nervous looks. Clover's ability to cry was legendary; if she began a full weepathon now, the party would be over before she was even halfway through her allotted box of tissues.

'Listen, I know it's frustrating having to wait for your presents . . .' Pea began.

'But it's loads more annoying for us,' said Tinkerbell. 'You *always* get yours before I get mine. Every year. For, like, the whole of my life for ever and ever and ever.'

This was true. Quite by chance, the Llewellyn family birthdays were all squeezed into the month of May. After Clover came Tinkerbell, who would be eight on the 13th. Pea (who would be turning twelve) and Mum shared a birthday, on the 28th. Every year, the flipping-over of the family calendar to May was greeted with cheers from the sisters, and groans from Mum, who had to pay for it all.

Secretly, Pea hated it. It wasn't the waiting she minded, exactly; she had always thought that the anticipation when faced with a pile of still-wrapped presents might be her very favourite part of a birthday. (She had a good imagination, and dreaming up what might be inside each lumpy package was always a thrill – when of course the real contents might well turn out to be socks.) But by the time Pea's big day arrived, everyone was fed up with parties and saying 'Ooh, how lovely' while other people unwrapped things. Everyone except Pea. Since it was Mum's birthday too, she never had a whole one to herself, either. This year, 28th May was also opening night for *Alice in Wonderland*, and since Clover was going to play Alice, she would have to share it even more than usual. Really, she thought, if anyone was entitled to lock themselves in their bedroom to sniffle and push rude notes under the door, it was her.

But it wasn't her birthday party today. It was Clover's, and it was almost ready to start, and as usual Pea would have to be the calm, sensible sister who mended everything.

'What's *that*?' said Tinkerbell, sniffing the air.

Pea wrinkled up her nose. There was a sort of crispy smell, like something being fried that shouldn't be.

The moment she recognized it, Pea gasped. 'Are you straightening your hair at the same time as having a big cry?' she said, hammering on the door much less sympathetically.

Another note slid out:

I'm
multi-
tasking

'Enough?' asked Tinkerbell.

'Enough,' said Pea firmly. She gripped the door handle, and pushed hard. 'Now shush up and listen, Clover, because— Oh!'

Standing in the centre of the orange-painted bedroom was Alice in Wonderland.

It was Clover really, of course. She was holding some hair-straighteners, which Pea was quite sure weren't in the original story, but otherwise she was dressed *exactly* like the drawings in the book on Pea's attic bookshelf. She wore a blue dress with a skirt that stuck out, a white pinny over the front, white socks and neat black shoes. Her long yellowy hair, usually so tumbly and wavy, now hung straight about her pink face, and there was a blue ribbon on the bed, waiting to sweep it back off her forehead.

'Is it all right?' said Clover, smoothing her skirts anxiously.

The school Drama Club had always been quite do-it-yourself with costumes, but now that Clover had joined Stage Right, a new weekend theatre school, everything was a touch more professional. It had made picking the theme for her birthday party easy (and finding props and costumes for everyone else even easier). Pea had seen the costume dangling from a hanger before – but seeing it all put together was quite different.

Even Tinkerbell seemed mesmerized. 'You look . . . fictional,' she murmured, eventually.

'In the good way,' Pea added, just in case.

Clover's pink face broke into a bright smile. '*Thank* you,' she said. 'I got panicked all of a sudden about whether a tea party was right, because what your birthday party's like is what *you're* like, isn't it? And Minta Prince had a disco, with boys. I am fourteen now – well, nearly – so I need to show off how mature and sophisticated I am. But I texted Tash, and Tash says that having the sort of birthday party with cakes and balloons and people bringing you presents is so retro and kiddy-like it's completely mature and sophisticated-seeming. Only by then I'd left it a bit too long to be able to come back downstairs without looking stupid, so I thought I might as well get dressed.'

'Fifteen minutes!' yelled Mum from downstairs.

Clover's eyes went wide.

'Don't panic,' said Pea, sensing another meltdown and shooing Clover out of the room before it could take hold. 'Me and Tink'll get changed, you go and help Mum with the food – and explain the dressing-up thing to Noelle again, because she still doesn't get it.'

Noelle was the family's new *au pair*. Ever since they'd moved to London, there had been an extra person living with them; a helper to take Tinkerbell to school and look after things while Mum was out teaching Creative Writing, or locked in her study dreaming up more mermaids. First there had been Vitória, who made coffee in tiny cups, and wondrous twirly hairdos. Their previous helper, Klaudia, wasn't officially an *au pair* at all, and had ended up living with them by accident. But she'd moved back into a student house almost a month ago, and now the room off the kitchen marked PRIVATE was occupied by a stranger.

Noelle was eighteen, and French. She had solemn grey eyes, but they were usually hidden behind two curtains of limp brown hair. Her most visible feature was her bony nose, the tip of which was always red from sniffling. When she'd first arrived, Pea assumed she must have a cold, but it had been two weeks, and still Noelle never went anywhere without a fistful of tissues and a damp air. She didn't let them wheel her in a trolley around Tesco, like Klaudia had. She didn't do twirly hairdos. Even her clothes seemed glum; all puddle colours, greys and browns. When Mum had explained, in slow, simple words – Noelle was still learning English – about the birthday party, and dressing up, Noelle had given her a mystified stare and simply said, '*Non*,' in her whisper-soft voice.

Mum said it was homesickness, and that they should be kind. They had been, mostly, apart from

Tinkerbell calling her 'Le Drip' behind her back. Clover was forever offering to lend her a scarf or a hat in cheerful red, or perky blue. Pea had even taken to writing her a series of tips, in instalments, to help her settle in.

A HELPFUL GUIDE TO BRITISH THINGS:

TEA

Tea is a very important British thing. If you are posh you might have a teapot and weird-smelling tea like Lapsang Souchong, and rules about whether to put the milk in first, but we are not posh. The only rules of tea are:

- mugs not cups
- milk (before or after, but always)
- smush the tea bag with a spoon till the tea is sort of orange – Mum likes it like that
- NO LEMONS

BREAKFAST

A 'full English breakfast' consists of:

- sausages
- bacon
- eggs (fried or scrambled or poached – poached is nicest)
- mushrooms
- tomatoes
- toast
- optional: black pudding (I'm not telling you what that is), baked beans, hash browns

British people NEVER eat this. Only as a treat or if they are on holiday. But if you wanted to learn how to make it. I don't think anyone would mind.

Noelle had at least stopped trying to put sour lemons in Mum's Special Writing Tea. But still, she wasn't much fun.

Pea quickly got changed in her attic bedroom at the top of the house, and by the time she came back downstairs, everything was almost ready.

The kitchen table was laid with the perfect Alice-themed afternoon tea: tiny sandwiches and sausage rolls, paper cups for lemonade with DRINK ME scrawled on the side, and jam tarts shaped like hearts. The table was decorated with paper roses, painted half red, half white. In the centre was a cake shaped like a teapot, with an edible handle and spout made of marzipan. (There had already been some discussion about who would get to eat those bits.)

In the garden, there was a game of not-quite-croquet laid out. (There weren't any hoops, and the mallets were a mixture of borrowed golf clubs and badminton rackets – but as Clover said, no one knew how to play croquet anyway, so it could hardly matter.)

The costumes – all borrowed from Stage Right

– were the best of all. To go with Clover's perfect Alice, Mum was the Mad Hatter, with a tall green foam hat that kept bumping into lampshades. Pea was the White Rabbit, her curly red hair swept back under a hairband with fluffy white ears. Tinkerbell was the Red Queen. (The Red Queen in the book wasn't a short almost-eight-year-old with brown skin, muddy trainers, and a magic wand made out of felt pens, but Tink was far too good at bellowing 'Off with her head!' to be anyone else.) Even Wuffly the dog was joining in as the Cheshire Cat, with a toothy cardboard smile tied to her collar.

Only Noelle was left un-birthday-fied.

'*Bonjour*, Le Drip!' said Tinkerbell, tapping on the door that led off the kitchen into the *au pair*'s private room. 'You have to be the Dormouse now, it's half-past three!'

'*Comment?*' murmured Noelle, opening the door just a crack so her bony nose poked out. A bony finger followed, pointing. 'What is . . . clotheses?'

'It's a costume party, remember?' said Clover,

17

twirling her skirt with pride. Then she pushed the door wider, reached up, and plonked two tufty brown ears onto Noelle's limp hair. 'And here's a furry nose on elastic. Now: whiskers?'

Tinkerbell advanced, eyeliner pencil in hand. 'Don't look so worried, I'm only going to draw on your face.'

With a squeak, Noelle recoiled and pushed the door shut. 'I tired. I studying now. I do not mouse,' she whimpered through the door.

The doorbell rang with the first of the guests.

'It's starting!' said Clover, frantically knocking on Noelle's door. 'Come out!'

'Um. In the book, the Dormouse is asleep at the tea party,' said Pea (who didn't mind wearing ears, but thought that people who didn't want to ought to be left alone). 'So if Noelle just stays in her room, she's being very lifelike, really.'

'We won't miss her – she never says anything anyway,' said Tinkerbell.

'Tink!' said Mum. 'Don't be so awful. You'd be

quiet too if you could only say things in French all day long. Get down, Wuffly! No one wants jam tarts that have been licked. Go on, Clover – answer the door!'

'Now, remember, everyone,' said Clover, 'you're not allowed to eat anything jammy or dribbly or likely to stain, or I'll get in trouble. And once my friends are all here, people younger than me have to go upstairs unless they're being useful and/or mature and sophisticated.'

First to arrive were Clover's best friends, Honey and Tash. They were both dressed as Alice too, though not as perfectly.

A trickle of other girls from Clover and Pea's school, Greyhope's, began to arrive, in ones and twos. Apart from one girl called Jules, who was wearing sparkly hot pants and looking quite self-conscious, they were all Alices.

'Laziness,' said Tinkerbell. 'Off with their heads!'

Pea braced herself for another weepathon, but

Clover didn't seem to mind. In fact she seemed quite pleased.

'It's as if they all want to be me,' she whispered to Pea.

Pea thought perhaps it was more that a blue dress and a hair ribbon was an easy costume to put together, but she didn't say so; it was Clover's party, after all.

The White Rabbit, the Red Queen and the Cheshire Cat dutifully sat on the stairs, near the top, watching and listening through the banisters.

The Alices ate all the jam tarts and the EAT ME cakes.

They gathered in the front room, and talked over the top of the *Alice in Wonderland* DVD: school gossip, oohs over Clover's tales of rehearsal drama, and a long debate on whether it would be worse to shrink down to a tiny person, or to grow enormous, if (unlike Alice) you were going to be stuck like that for ever. (The Alices all thought being smaller would be best, until Clover pointed out the chances of being trodden on, or licked to death by Wuffly, compared with being a giant who could stomp around and never ever be told off by anyone because you could just step on them. After that the other Alices all very much wanted to be massive.)

Then they went out into the garden.

Pea and Tinkerbell were beckoned into the kitchen, where Mum had kept a secret supply of jam tarts.

'Can we have not-quite-croquet at *my* birthday party?' asked Tinkerbell, watching out of the window as plastic golf balls sailed past at random.

'I thought you wanted the Amazing Sylvester to come and do magic tricks?' said Mum.

'I do. Definitely and absolutely. But maybe my party could have both. And jelly. I definitely want jelly.'

Mum smiled. 'One magic-, croquet- and jelly-themed party coming up. What about you, Pea-pod? We'll be going to Clover's play in the evening, obviously – but you could have a daytime party before that, or bring some friends to the play?'

'I haven't decided yet,' said Pea.

Last year they'd had fish and chips and silly games on Tenby beach, just like the year before. But this year would be different: Londonish, new, something perfectly Pea-like. She just couldn't decide what.

When a near-fight broke out over the rules of not-quite-croquet, Mum tinged her spoon against a teacup, and brought everyone indoors.

On the kitchen table was a small pile of presents from various Alices, which Clover would be allowed to open today. Beside it, the iced teapot now had fourteen candles poked into its marzipan lid, all flickering away.

Clover's face glowed in the candlelight, her eyes shining. Pea felt a magical birthday tingling feeling creep across her skin. She didn't mind coming last, or having to share with Mum, and Clover's play, not really; not when birthdays were so lovely. Less than a month to wait, and she would be blowing out her own candles . . .

As everyone – even Noelle, without the mouse ears – gathered around the table to sing 'Happy Birthday', the phone rang.

'Sorry, darling!' mouthed Mum, hurrying to pick it up as the Alices began to sing.

'Happy birthday . . .'

Pea watched Mum pick up the phone, taking off her hat and putting one finger in her ear so she could hear over the singing.

'Happy birthday . . .'

It would be Clem calling to wish Clover a happy birthday, Pea was sure. Clem was only Tinkerbell's dad, technically, not hers or Clover's, but he felt real and dad-like to all of them. This was the first May since they'd moved away from Tenby; the first year he hadn't been able to pop over on the day and give one of them a present and a kiss in person. Pea glanced at Clover, and saw a flicker of something sad cross her eyes in the candlelight, as if she'd just that moment thought the same thing.

'*Dear Clover . . .*'

Clover blinked, and smiled the worry away. But when Pea looked over at Mum, she wasn't smiling. She had her hand clamped over her mouth, and her eyes were stretched out wide and upset.

'Hip-hip-hooray!' shouted Tinkerbell.

The Alices joined in, and Clover blew out her candles to a glorious round of applause – but as it died away, they could all hear Mum's wobbly voice on the phone, saying, 'Yes, yes, I see. Thank you for calling.' When she put the phone down, a big tear rolled down her cheek and plopped on the floor.

'Mum?' said Clover.

'Oh, I'm so sorry,' Mum said, wiping away another tear. 'And in the middle of your party, Clover. It's Granny Duff, my starlings. She's died.'

A SAD DAY

All the Alices were sent home early. The presents were put in a corner, unopened. It was the worst possible end to a party, Pea thought – and then felt guilty for caring about parties when someone had died. Mum had told them Granny Duff wasn't well ages ago, she remembered, and said they must get around to visiting. But they hadn't. Pea had forgotten all about it.

Once the guests were all gone, Mum opened her arms and wrapped all three sisters up in a comforting, jasmine-perfume-smelling hug. Pea's White Rabbit ears got knocked sideways, and she tugged them off at once, blushing.

'I suppose we could still cut the cake,' said Mum, wanly looking at the spread on the kitchen table. 'It might cheer us up.'

'No!' said Clover. 'It would be like we're celebrating.'

'Or like we're giving Granny Duff a nice cheery wave goodbye?' said Tinkerbell, eyeing the marzipan spout. 'Made of cake?'

Pea shook her head. 'I think it might spoil birthday cakes for ever, to eat it now.'

Wuffly padded in, her collar still bearing the Cheshire Cat smile. Somehow it made it all seem even sadder. They agreed the cake would be best saved for later.

Noelle blew her nose. 'So,' she said, in a damp voice. 'It is the grandmother of who, this dead woman?'

Mum opened her mouth to reply. But it was as if the question had opened up a door in her head that let all the sadness out. With a sob and a

26

mumble about 'popping upstairs for a moment', she fled.

Noelle blinked solemnly through her hair. Then she tapped the table, frowning. 'Explain me! Who is dead woman?'

'Stop saying *dead woman!*' snapped Pea, tears pricking at her eyes now too.

Clover squeezed Pea's arm, and Tinkerbell's. Then they all sat around the table, amongst the empty DRINK ME cups and leftover jam tarts. Clover cleared her throat, and launched into the familiar old story about their dads. She said it extra-slowly and with simpler words, in case Noelle found it hard to follow.

'When Mum was young – about your age actually, Noelle – she fell in love with a boy called Dave Duff, and they had a baby.'

'The baby was Clover,' added Tinkerbell.

'Yes,' said Clover. 'And they were very happy, only Dave got killed in a motorbike accident when I was still only tiny, which is awful, isn't it?

Mum was very sad, I expect – I mean, I was a baby so I don't remember. But she decided that it meant that life is too short to waste on being boring, so she took my dad's life insurance money – that's money you get if someone dies in an accident, Noelle – and bought a plane ticket to go travelling.'

Pea wasn't sure Noelle was really following the story, but Clover carried on anyway.

'She went to lots of different places with me, like India – I don't remember that, either – and then she went to the Greek Islands, and fell in love with a man called Ewan McGregor. Not the famous actor Ewan McGregor. Just an American man with the same name. And then she had another baby.'

'The baby was Pea,' added Tinkerbell.

Pea smiled, and gave Noelle a small wave.

'But the night Pea was born,' said Clover, dropping her voice to a whisper to add drama, 'he ran away and has never been heard from since. Isn't that tragic, Noelle?'

'We think he might have been a pirate,' said Tinkerbell.

'We don't really,' said Pea, her cheeks going pink. 'I mean, it's not exactly likely. But we don't know anything at all about him, so we can't rule it out.'

Noelle swept one hair curtain away from one solemn grey eye, and regarded her with new interest. Pea glowed. People assumed she must be sad about an absent father, but Pea had never minded; she felt he gave her an exotic air of mystery.

'Anyway,' said Clover, 'then Mum and me and Pea did lots and lots more travelling, and lived all over the world – in a commune in Germany, and on a houseboat in Norway, and a tent in Prestatyn; wherever Mum could find a place to stay. And then she met Clem, who's Jamaican, though he's from Birmingham really, and we moved to Tenby, and then Mum had another baby.'

'Me!' said Tinkerbell, waving her wand.

'And then last summer we all moved to London.

Only not Clem, because he doesn't live with us any more.'

Noelle shook her head. 'I understand. You are very strange family. But who is . . .' She was going to say *dead woman* again, then flicked her grey eyes warily at Pea. 'Who is . . . *dead person*?'

It wasn't any better, Pea thought, but at least she'd tried.

'Granny Duff was my grandmother,' said Clover. 'Dave Duff's mum, she would've been.'

Noelle nodded slowly. 'So. This Granny Duff: she is living in London?'

'No,' said Clover, 'she lives in – I mean, lived in . . . um . . .'

Pea and Tinkerbell both looked equally blank.

'Hereford,' said Mum, reappearing at the kitchen door. Her eyes were red, but she managed a smile. 'Granny Duff used to live in Wales, Noelle, near to where I grew up, but she moved to Hereford years ago. We used to visit, um, every now and then.'

'It was a big white house, wasn't it?' said Clover, frowning hard. 'With one of those square hedges along the front?'

'I remember,' said Pea, nodding. She had dim memories of sitting on the edge of a very stiff sofa, drinking too-weak blackcurrant squash out of a glass, and worrying about spilling it on the cream carpet. 'We used to go once a year, at Christmas time. She always had a really big tree in the window, with posh decorations all one colour.'

'I don't remember that,' said Tinkerbell.

Mum sighed. 'You probably wouldn't, my starling. Granny Duff and me – well, I wouldn't want to say anything unkind now the poor lady's gone, but we weren't friends, exactly. She was never very happy about Dave and me having a baby so young. After he died, I went off travelling, and took her only grandchild with me. Then I had more children, and that made things a bit complicated. She was never very interested in poor Pea and Tink, I'm afraid – so we didn't visit all that often.'

'What did she look like?' asked Tinkerbell. 'Because I'm imagining a grannyish sort of lady with red hair giving me sweets, but I think she might actually be Rita off *Coronation Street.*'

Mum gave Tinkerbell a watery smile. Then she went upstairs to root about in a cupboard for a picture of Granny Duff.

They spent the evening cuddled up on the sofa, going through old photograph albums. There was a tatty blue one full of Mum, when she was impossibly small. It had a snap tucked into the back page too: Mum as a blurry beaming teenage girl, her tummy full of Clover, her arms wrapped around the neck of a thin, dark-haired boy in unfashionable jeans.

The next album was all Clover as a fat pink baby.

The third held lots of bright prints of small Clover and Pea holding a tiny squirmy Tinkerbell, while Mum and Clem (looking much thinner than he did now) looked on fondly. There were pictures of Wuffly as a puppy too, though most of them were blurry; she had taken a long time to learn 'sit', 'roll over', and 'don't chew the camera'.

'We're missing a big chunk of our memory box,' Mum explained to Noelle. 'All that moving around when they were little made it hard to hang onto things – and then there was The Flood,' she added, with a shudder. 'We were living in this tiny flat in Amsterdam, and one day we came back and everything was underwater.'

Pea wrinkled up her nose at the memory of her drawing of a giraffe (mounted on green sugar paper, with a tick and a silver star sticker) as it floated by. At nursery she'd had to wear slippers as shoes; ones with the Incredible Hulk on, from the lost property box. Clover's beloved Wendy Doll had drowned. It wasn't until later that Mum realized that all Pea's baby photos had drowned too.

Suddenly Noelle let out an enormous sob.

'Oh, don't!' said Pea. 'I know it's awful, but I don't mind that much!'

'*Non,*' said Noelle huskily. 'I not worry for you.

33

I sad for my family. I have a homesick.'

'Oh,' said Pea. She really didn't mind for herself – like her pirate father, it made her feel mysterious, as if she might have been found at the foot of a beanstalk or carved from wood – but she thought Noelle might have cared a little bit. But Mum gave Noelle a pat on the arm, and asked if she'd like to share some family photos too.

Noelle nodded sourly, and returned with her laptop.

Apparently Noelle's family was large (there were lots of aunts, and cats), and her mother was a keen photographer: there was an album for every year of Noelle's life.

Two cups of tea later, when they had reached the album where Noelle was seven, Mum yawned meaningfully, and Noelle promised to show them the rest another time.

'Isn't it funny?' said Tinkerbell to Pea that night as they padded upstairs to bed. 'I've seen more of Le Drip as a baby now than I'll ever see of you.'

A Sad Day

Sunday 1 May

Dear Diary,
Granny Duff's funeral will be on Thursday.
That's Clover's birthday, which isn't very nice,
but Mum says it's not like it's very nice for
Granny Duff either and it can't be helped.

I don't think I want to go to a funeral. I do
care an awful lot about her being dead and
everything, but I already feel sad, and spending
a whole Thursday on being even more sad
doesn't seem like it will make any difference,
really. The only funeral I've ever been to before
was for a goldfish, but probably a person one
is different.

I asked Mum, and she said that Granny Duff
was our last link to Clover's dad's side of the
family, and it wasn't very nice of us not to have
visited her for so long, so we all absolutely
definitely have to go. Then she had a little cry.

I took her a slice of cake and a big piece of

marzipan teapot handle. That cheered her up lots.

I don't know what to do when we run out of cake, though.

Monday 2 May

Dear Diary,

Everyone at school was very kind, but not very helpful about what funerals are like. Eloise's grandpa died when she was too little to go to his funeral. Molly's grandparents are all alive and living in Marbella. I don't know about Bethany because she was showing me her new 1-Click Dream pencil case. I've never heard of 1-Click Dream, but they are boys, there are three of them and they have swooshy hair.

I thought I might find a book to help, but most of the ones on my shelf are about tragic orphans, who are generally post-funeral.

Tuesday 3 May

Dear Diary,
I asked Miss Pond, the school librarian, for some sad death books. She looked at me a bit funny and sent me to see Acting Deputy Head Mrs King about my 'morbid tendencies', but Mum had already explained why we needed to have Thursday off school so she was quite understanding and tried to hug me.

Miss Pond gave me *The Cat Mummy*, *Ways to Live Forever*, and *Bridge to Terabithia* to read. I am alternating chapters with re-reading one of Mum's *Mermaid Girls* books, in case morbid tendencies strike.

I feel very sad. But also a bit excited about my birthday. I hope that's allowed.

Wednesday 4 May

Dear Diary,
I went to Bethany's house after school. Her

bedroom used to have horse posters all over the walls, but now it is all pictures of 1-Click Dream. Apparently they are a band. She played me three of their videos, lots of times. Her favourite one is the short one with the swooshiest hair. I don't have a favourite one, but Bethany says that's because I'm younger than her and when I stop being eleven I'll change.

I'm a bit less excited about my birthday now. I like my bedroom the way it is.

On Thursday morning, instead of putting on the browns and yellows of her Greyhope's uniform, Pea wore dark grey jeans and a black top.

Noelle was staying behind to look after Wuffly. They would take the train to Hereford, then a taxi to the funeral, and be back by the evening. And, Mum promised, Clover could do something lovely the next night to make up for her unhappy birthday. (Tinkerbell's protest that she was having *three* birthdays now fell on deaf ears.)

They boarded the train at Paddington, and had four seats round a table, with cardboard labels stuck in the back to show they were reserved.

Clover took out her script, and began to read her lines over to herself (first out loud, and then, after a stern look from Mum, just moving her lips).

Tinkerbell wrote her party invitations. They were special printed ones, with a picture of a rabbit popping out of a hat to hold the bit where you wrote the name and time.

'There are matching party bags too,' said Tinkerbell, noticing Pea eyeing the design. 'If there's any left over, you can have them for your party, I promise.'

'That's sweet, Stinks, but Pea's a bit old for all that,' said Mum, giving Pea a fond look.

Pea nodded slowly. Bethany and Eloise hadn't done party bags at their birthdays, now she thought about it. It seemed that wanting to take home a slice of cake with the jam and icing all glued to the napkin wrapper was something you were supposed to grow out of, like horse posters, once you were mature and sophisticated.

It seemed a shame (Pea really liked cake), but it was a little bit thrilling to imagine herself grown-up: taller, Clover-like. (Imaginary grown-up Pea also had a smaller chin, somehow.)

She took out her rainbow notebook, the one she did all her creative writing in. She'd planned to spend the journey writing the latest story in her *A Girl Called Sky* series, all about a girl (called Sky) who lived on the moon.

One morning, Sky yawned, stretched, and jumped out of bed to get ready for space school. She thought it was just another ordinary day on the moon – but when she looked in her space mirror, her whole face had turned green, with dark green spots.

'I've seen these symptoms before,' said Doctor Prism. 'You have Mashed Potato Poisoning!'

But instead of continuing the story, Pea turned to a fresh page, and made a list of Mature and Sophisticated Things to try out.

M & S Things

Conversation: talk more about school, hair, deep philosophical questions – e.g. would it be better to be suddenly very small or suddenly massive?

Fashion: care about this.

Food: eat frondy lettuce, only eat two squares of chocolate and save the rest of the bar for another day, use correct knife and fork (not sure about this as there is only one knife and fork normally).

Pea chewed the end of her pencil, then added, with a sigh:

Probably no Pot Noodles.

Being mature and sophisticated was going to be quite a challenge.

Mum's phone rang about an hour into the journey. It was a journalist from *London Now*; Mum had met her last week for an interview, and to have her picture taken all dressed up as Marina Cove. Apparently the journalist had some extra questions, which Mum started to answer – until Clover gave *her* a stern look, and she scurried along the train to finish the interview outside the toilet.

Pea tried to concentrate on her library book. But as they got closer and closer to Hereford, she forgot all about birthdays and started to feel panicky. The books she'd read so far all had different ideas of what a funeral was like. Would there be a coffin, with a body in it? Would she be one of the people they asked to carry it? Would Mum cry? Would *she* cry? Would people be cross if she *didn't* cry? She was so nervous about doing something wrong, she couldn't eat a mouthful of their on-the-train picnic – not even leftover teapot cake.

But it turned out that her worries were all for nothing. She'd imagined a huge gothic cathedral and a scary vicar – but instead the service was held in a small modern building. There were flowers, and a little huddle of people dressed in black, but no spooky organ music, and no coffin either. A woman with grey hair got up and read a poem about *going away to a silent land*, which made Clover sob. Another woman said a little bit about Granny Duff – or Glenda, which was her real name – who had apparently done all sorts of things in her life that Pea had never thought of, like being young, and getting married twice, and working as a pharmacist in the chemist's on Abergavenny

High Street. When she told stories about that part, some people laughed, which Pea thought was very shocking – but Mum whispered that laughing was definitely allowed at a funeral.

Afterwards all the people who'd been at the funeral went to a pub. There were sandwiches, and sausage rolls, and even jam tarts.

'Like Clover's tea party,' murmured Tinkerbell, looking as surprised as Pea.

'It's called a wake,' said Clover knowledgeably. 'You always have one after a funeral. It's meant to cheer everyone up again after all the weeping.'

Mum didn't look very cheerful, but she and Clover chatted to the lady who'd talked about the chemist's shop (who was apparently some complicated sort of cousin), and introduced themselves to a few other people. Pea suspected that joining in would be the mature and sophisticated thing to do – but it had been a long day, so she sat in a corner with Tinkerbell, eating sausage rolls instead.

'I'm so sorry, my doves,' said Mum, once they

were on the train home. 'I thought Granny Duff would go on for ever, the way people do. And I know we didn't get on, but family's a part of who you are; it's important to know where you come from. I'm sorry if you've missed out on a bit of our family history.'

'*Clover*'s family history, you mean,' said Tinkerbell.

'That's not how our family works, is it?' said Mum with a frown. 'Remember all the times we went up to Birmingham to see Clem's mum, and his nana, and his brothers and all the little cousins? They're still part of our family, and we're part of theirs – *all* of us. We're all Llewellyns, but we're Duffs and Thompsons as well.'

'And McGregors,' added Pea.

Mum tilted her head, and stroked Pea's ponytail. 'Yes, that too, I suppose. A bit of the pirate in all of us.'

Then she laughed – a melancholy laugh, Pea thought – and drummed her fingers on the armrest.

Pea chewed the inside of her cheek, thinking. If it was important to know where you come from, having a mysterious pirate dad was a bit inconvenient. She didn't know anything at all about him, apart from his name, and that he was an American who had once lived on a Greek island. She didn't even know which Greek island it had been.

But before she could wonder about it out loud, Mum discovered the jam tarts – now covered in blue fluff – that had ended up in Tinkerbell's coat pocket, and the rest of the journey was spent in apologetic silence.

'The dog, she was sick,' Noelle announced in a dull voice when they got home.

No one felt much like celebrating Clover's birthday.

But the next morning Clover woke them all up early so she could unwrap presents before school, and then she had a sleepover party with Tash, Honey, and a selection of Alices. Mum and Noelle covered the front-room floor with duvets and pillows, and made popcorn.

Pea, Tinkerbell and Wuffly were banished to the kitchen – although Pea kept popping her nose in and offering to take away empty glasses, so she could observe a truly mature and sophisticated birthday in action. It looked bearable. They didn't seem to be doing anything, really, apart from giggling and painting each other's toenails.

'I think everyone should have at least two birthdays,' said Clover, on a lemonade run to the fridge. She was wearing her best spotty pyjamas, and her hair was in lopsided plaits, courtesy of Tash. 'Though for nicer reasons, obviously. Oh, is that for me?'

There was a battered brown envelope – the padded sort, for small parcels – on the kitchen counter, addressed to Clover.

'It arrives late,' said Noelle, glumly picking pineapple off her pizza slice. 'After midday. The postman, he is very bad.'

Clover ripped it open. Inside was a small birthday card and a badly wrapped present.

'Oh! It's from Granny Duff,' she said, in an odd voice.

Pea bit her lip. It was an impossible letter, sent by someone who they'd never see again. Inside that card were Granny Duff's last words – to them, at least. She peered over Clover's shoulder to read.

Dearest Clover,
I've been sorting through some old things (by the time you get this, I expect you'll know why), and I found this. It belonged to your daddy, who was given it by his own grandfather. I think he would like you to have it.
Happy birthday, my darling.
All my love,
Granny

'Unwrap it, unwrap it,' said Tinkerbell, hopping.

With fumbly fingers, Clover pulled off all the sticky tape and paper, to reveal a small squarish box. She flipped it open.

Inside was a watch. It had a brown leather strap, and a large face with roman numerals on an ivory background. The hands were silver. Clover held it to Pea's ear, so she could hear the tick.

'Oh!' said Mum, arriving in the kitchen with her empty tea mug. She reached out to pick up the watch, then hesitated, and drew her hand back. 'Oh,' she said again, blinking a lot as she read the card.

Clover put it on, struggling a little with the fastening. It looked very big on her small wrist.

'We can get a new strap for it,' said Mum, 'or maybe get it made into a necklace or something, if you didn't want to wear it as a watch?'

But Clover held her arm out admiringly, and shook her head. 'It's perfect just as it is,' she said. 'My first ever birthday present from my dad.'

CHAPTER 3

THE MAKE-IT-
BETTER LETTERS

Dear Clem,

Here is all our news from London.
• I have been to my first funeral (not counting
fish). It wasn't too awful, but I'd prefer not to go
to one again for a long time.
• Noelle is going to have extra English lessons
with a girl called Tansy, who is a friend of
Klaudia's from university. Tansy is American, but
I have watched a lot of episodes of *iCarly* so I
should be able to translate.

• Clover's production of *Alice in Wonderland* might not be happening because Stage Right haven't got a director. (They had one but she's got shingles. I don't know what that is but it stops you from doing plays, anyway.) Clover has offered to direct it herself. Mum said she'd find it too hard to tell herself off if she did any bad acting, and Clover said she wouldn't ever do any bad acting, and Mum said 'Exactly.' So I don't think that will work.

• Tinkerbell has invited your mum and Uncle Joe and Uncle Cliff and all the little cousins to her birthday party as well as you, because we have been thinking a lot about families, and making sure we talk to them all. At least, everyone else has.

• The Amazing Sylvester is coming to do magic tricks, but I'm not sure if he's actually amazing or if that's just his name, so don't worry if they can't come. (Tink has also invited 29 people from her school, so if they do come they might have to sit

51

on the floor because we definitely haven't got that many chairs.)

• I haven't decided what kind of party I'm going to have so you haven't got an invitation from me yet, but it will be mature and sophisticated and there might be toenail-painting.

• Have you ever been to a Greek island? I'm just wondering what they're like.

We miss you!
Love from Pea xx

On Saturday, Clover went off to her directorless *Alice in Wonderland* rehearsal, grumbling all the way. Pea and Tinkerbell went to see their next-door neighbours.

The Paget-Skidelskys were two mums and two Sams. The Sams weren't identical twins, but they did look incredibly alike – floppy brown hair and thin freckled faces. Sam One was a boy, and the one Pea liked best; they wrote stories and comics together – Sam One did the pictures. Sam Two was the girl twin, who Pea found a bit harder to like; she had been known to 'accidentally' spill her orange juice all over Space Ant's adventures just when Pea and Sam One had got to the very last page, and not look particularly sorry about it either. Tinkerbell, however, thought she was brilliant.

As usual, the moment the door opened, they were greeted by a bouncy bundle of hairy grey puppy. The puppy was named Surprise, and in the weeks since his arrival he'd been determined to live up to it, endlessly leaving small 'surprises' in puddles around the house.

Tinkerbell was supposed to be helping Sam Two teach him to behave better. The pair took Surprise into the piano room right away, equipped with a freshly mended magic wand, for his next round of puppy-training. (From what Pea could hear through the window, this involved very little 'sit', or 'roll over', and a lot of 'bite Mum K!' and

'*Puppyo vanisho!*' – although Surprise seemed to ignore all commands equally.)

Pea and Sam One sat at the coffee table, working on their latest comic, *The Castle of Fright*. It was the tale of a young girl named Amethyst (Amy for short) who got lost on the way home one dark night, and ended up sleeping in a spooky castle. So far she'd met a friendly bat called Batthew, and nothing very terrifying had happened apart from some creaky floorboards and the occasional spider. Pea had been looking forward to getting back to it – but she found herself going quieter and quieter as Sam One enthusiastically drew gravestones all around the castle walls. It was perhaps not the ideal story to be writing, under the circumstances.

'Oh dear,' said Dr Paget, noticing Pea looking rather sick. 'Perhaps you two could do some more *Space Ant* today, instead? Perhaps *Space Ant Goes on a Picnic and Has a Relaxing Time Where Nothing Very Bad Happens at All*?'

Sam One frowned, then looked at the skeleton he was halfway through drawing. 'Sorry,' he said, and quickly rubbed it out.

'Thanks,' murmured Pea.

'Don't you tell your clients that it's healthiest for children to confront the subject of death head-on, hmm?' said Dr Skidelsky, lowering her book and looking at Dr Paget reproachfully over the top of her oblong glasses.

Dr Genevieve Paget and Dr Kara Skidelsky were Family Therapists and Child Psychologists; it said so on a gold plaque on the pillar at the end of their path. Dr Skidelsky spent her weekdays in Edinburgh, teaching at the university and writing an important book about childhood (lots of which was apparently based on the Sams). She had spiky hair and wore Wonder Woman T-shirts, but was definitely the more serious one. Dr Paget did the actual therapy, talking to upset people on the plush golden sofas in their front room. Pea could see why: she was long and thin, but there was something

55

soft about her smile that made her ever so easy to talk to.

'I think going to a funeral is more than enough confronting!' said Dr Paget, not very softly at all. Then she sighed, and fiddled with her string of beads. 'Though I suppose you have a point. Pea, if any of you want to talk about your grandmother, we're here. A death in the family is a big challenge, emotionally. You mustn't bottle anything up. And I imagine your mum's got a lot on her plate, coping with the news herself.'

'That's all right, Mum didn't like Granny Duff anyway,' said Tinkerbell casually, following Sam Two back into the room.

'Tink!' said Pea.

'Furniture!' said Dr Skidelsky as Surprise bounded in after them and jumped onto an armchair, immediately beginning to savage a cushion.

Sam Two grabbed Surprise's favourite toy – a squeaky orange carrot with a face on it

– and waved it under his nose, cooing, 'Here, silly doggy,' until he hopped down to chew on that instead.

'Or maybe it was the other way round,' said Tinkerbell. 'They weren't friends, anyway.'

Pea's face felt hot. She looked pleadingly at Dr Paget. 'She doesn't mean . . . It's just that . . .'

'You don't have to explain,' said Dr Skidelsky, with an unexpected grin. 'Families are the people you love, but you don't always *like* them.'

'You like us, don't you?' said Sam Two.

It was Dr Paget's turn to give Dr Skidelsky a reproachful look.

'Of course,' said Dr Skidelsky. 'Always. But we might not always like your *behaviour*. In the same way that you, Sam, love that ridiculous animal – but you aren't necessarily thrilled when it wees on your bed.'

Surprise's ears pricked up, and he scampered across the room to pant expectantly at Dr Skidelsky. She gave him a wary look, but Surprise went on wagging his tail until Dr Skidelsky grimaced, and gave his head an awkward pat. (Dr Skidelsky was not a fan of dogs. While Sam Two was training Surprise to be a good puppy, Surprise was meant to be training Dr Skidelsky to be a good human. They were making slow progress.)

'Well put,' said Dr Paget. 'Even if your mum and your grandmother weren't best friends, I'm sure they meant a lot to one another. In fact, I expect your mum probably wishes they'd been closer, now.'

Pea nodded. 'She said it's her fault we've missed out on some of our family history.'

Dr Paget sighed. 'Many people feel regretful after a death. All the things they should've said, or done, and now it's too late. Although it doesn't have to be. I offer therapy to bereaved clients, and we do a lot of letter-writing. If there are things they feel they should've said, they put them all in a letter. I call them Make-It-Better Letters.'

'Even if the person they're writing to is dead?'

said Tinkerbell, scrunching up her nose. 'Who do you post it to?'

'You don't post the letter,' said Dr Paget with a smile. 'Of course, some people believe that a dead person's spirit, or soul, is still around, and might read the words – but that's not the point. You write it for you: to make *you* feel better, so no one else needs to see it. It works for lots of problems, actually. If a grown-up couple have come to see me because they're arguing a lot, they sometimes find it easier to work out why if they write it down, calmly. They might write a long list of moany things about how their husband never puts the milk back in the fridge or their wife leaves tea bags in the sink – and right down at the bottom of the list they'll have put something enormous, like wanting to have a baby, only they never have that conversation because they fight about the small things instead. Children sometimes write letters to their parents. I even get people to write letters to themselves, if they're depressed, and need to think of reasons to like themselves again. Often it's not until you've written it down that you realize what you're feeling.'

Pea nodded. Being a writer herself, she knew exactly what Dr Paget meant. For a while, not long ago, she'd given up on her diary, and her weekly email to Clem, and lost all track of herself.

They stayed for lunch: carrot soup with ginger in it, which was so spicy it made the inside of Pea's nose feel hot and itchy – but spicy things were definitely M & S, so she ate it anyway.

Then, much to Tinkerbell's disgust, Sam Two had to go for football practice with her team, the Kensal Rise Kites. (Tinkerbell had to wait for her eighth birthday to be able to join; it was now only six days away, but according to Tinkerbell, the nearer it came, the slower the days seemed to go.) They waved goodbye to Surprise as he cheerfully lifted his leg and did a wee on Dr Skidelsky's briefcase, then headed home.

Clover had arrived just before them, beaming and filled with good news.

'We've got a director after all! He's called Mr Kovacic, but he says we can call him Marko, because we shouldn't be formal if we're going on a journey to the core of our personalities together. He wears slinky trousers like your fancy pyjamas, Mum, and he's got a very deep voice, and he's given me a whole list of exercises to help me *find* Alice. We're starting rehearsals all over again. He says he wants our production to explore the savage emotional underbelly of Wonderland. Doesn't that sound amazing?'

Pea didn't think somewhere called Wonderland was really meant to have a savage emotional underbelly, but at least Clover was happy.

Mum had good news too.

'Remember the interview I did? Look!' She held up a copy of *London Now* with a grin.

They all gathered around the coffee table to read. Pea flipped past the adverts till she found

61

a photograph of Mum, looking slightly more beautiful than was quite normal. There were pictures of her book covers too. The headline said:

MERMAIDS BY DAY, MUM BY NIGHT.
Meet the real superwoman: she's even got a secret identity. If your little girl loves a sparkly mermaid book, she's guaranteed to have read and loved Marina Cove's *Mermaid Girls*. But Marina is really single mum of three Brie Llewellyn. We sat down with Brie to talk parenting, London life, and how to make your own writing dreams come true . . .

'They've spelled your name wrong,' said Clover.

'Oh, I know,' said Mum. (Mum's real name was Bree Llewellyn – not Brie like the cheese – but the Dreaditor had decided that Marina Cove was a much simpler name to put on a book cover. Now they could see why.) 'It's a sweet little interview otherwise, don't you think?'

Pea read carefully, past a boring part describing Mum's clothes and shoes, and where she liked to go shopping. There was a nice bit about all three sisters being always at the heart of Mum's story ideas; that made her glow with pride. At the end there was a bit more about Mum's writing.

As her inspirational children grow up, is she tempted to branch out into older fiction, I wonder – perhaps even writing for adults?

Brie won't say, though there's a definite twinkle in her eye as she talks about the future. 'I'm redrafting the fifth *Mermaid Girls* book right now, and loving it as always. But I can't write about mermaids for ever.'

Intriguing stuff. Whenever 'Marina Cove' decides to hang up her tail, we're sure Brie Llewellyn will be a name to watch.

'Oh!' gasped Pea. Her fingertips shot to her mouth automatically, and pressed against her lips.

Mum was still looking at her expectantly, so Pea made her lips back into a smile.

'Sweet, yes,' she said.

But it wasn't what she was thinking at all.

That night, they had beans on toast with grated cheese melted on the top for tea. (Noelle took one sniff, and made herself an omelette instead. Pea watched enviously as she whisked the eggs in the bowl, wishing she'd thought to turn up her nose at beans too.) Then Mum went off to the cinema with Dr Paget. Pea and Tinkerbell took Wuffly out for a quick dash around the block, then the three sisters flopped on the new red sofa that Mum had finally found to replace their wheezy inflatable Hannah Montana one.

Tinkerbell fetched a notepad and began to write, her feet resting on Wuffly's hairy back. Clover watched a TV show about medieval dresses and kissing. Pea borrowed Clover's hair straighteners, and tried out having flat hair instead of frizzy while she watched too – but after ten minutes she'd achieved nothing but tired arms and a very hot ponytail. Clover tried taking over, but in the end they concluded that Pea had magic hair that refused to be uncurly.

'Like Tink's,' said Clover. 'Well, ish. Maybe you should try out her CurlyGurl coconut stuff?'

Tinkerbell had her own special hair goop, applied once a week to reduce fluffiness. Judging by her fierce glare, she was not keen to share - but Pea had already decided not to bother; magic hair sounded like quite a good thing to have.

Noelle brought in hot chocolate – in bowls, French-style – arranged on a tray. 'What is this?' she asked, pointing at Tinkerbell's notepad.

'I'm writing a Better Letter to Granny Duff,' said Tinkerbell.

'Oh, Tink,' said Clover, turning the sound down on the TV and squeezing her arm. 'I thought you understood. When someone dies, they're gone: they don't come back.'

But Pea explained about Dr Paget's idea of writing all the things you hadn't said to someone, even if they never got to read it.

Clover's eyes lit up. She fetched a pen and borrowed some of Tinkerbell's paper. 'I'm going to write to my dad,' she said. 'To say thank you for my birthday watch, and that I wish I remembered him. And that I hope they have nicer jeans in heaven, or wherever he is.'

'Angels don't wear jeans,' said Tinkerbell. 'They wear dresses made out of sheets – we did it at school.'

They both fell silent, pens scratching away as they wrote.

Pea borrowed some of Tinkerbell's paper too. After careful thought, she'd decided Mum couldn't possibly be allowed to stop writing the *Mermaid Girls* books. Pea had read them over and over again – and Mum always asked for help brainstorming new ideas whenever she hit a sticky point. The mermaid feast of eel spaghetti and seaweed salad in the second book had been completely Pea's invention. Every time she read that page, she felt a tingly thrill at seeing something *she'd* invented, actually printed in a book. It wasn't quite the same as having her own name on the spine; that was her real dream. But it did nicely for now. It was something special they did together, just Mum and Pea.

Besides, at the end of book five the ghost of Coraly had commanded a sea monster to squish the Dread Pirate Ellis with its tentacles, but on the very last page Shelley had seen a ghostly ship reflected in the melting ice around Snowflake Island, as if perhaps the Dread Pirate Ellis might not be so squished after all . . . She couldn't stop when there was a cliffhanger like that.

If Pea could come up with some brilliant – and, of course, mature and sophisticated – ideas, Mum would have to keep writing mermaid stories.

What if Lorelei grew up and got a job working as a journalist doing the TV news, and she had to keep her mermaidness a big secret, only sometimes there would be news stories in the water?

What if Shelley invented underwater mermaid hair-straighteners that ran on a new special kind of electricity, and she became a millionaire?

What if they opened a posh restaurant serving frondy lettuce, with extra forks?

They weren't awful ideas – but she wasn't sure they were as good as eel spaghetti. They weren't much like Clover's TV show about dresses and kissing, either. And it was hard to concentrate on mermaids when her brain kept drifting back to what Mum had said on the train – about how important it was to know where you'd come from. Tinkerbell's magic hair came from Clem. Clover had her watch, and a Granny who'd worked in a chemist's in Abergavenny. Pea didn't have anything like that; only stories about a pirate on a faraway island. There wasn't even a photograph of him in horrible jeans.

Dr Paget had said it didn't need to be a dead person that you wrote to.

Switching off the unwatched TV, Pea asked Tinkerbell for another piece of paper. Then she chewed on the end of the pen, thinking.

It was hard to get started, but once she had, there seemed to be a lot to say.

Dear Ewan McGregor,

I hope you don't mind me calling you that instead of 'Dad', only I've never called anyone Dad and it feels too peculiar.

I've never written you a letter before, but now there are some things I would like to ask.

- Are you a pirate?
- Why did you run away when I was born? (Was it something I did or was it about Mum? Or do you just not like babies very much? If it was not liking babies, I'm nearly 12 now.)
- If you are American, then does that mean I'm half American?
- Does having red hair and a big chin run in your family?
- Are people mean about it, and do you have useful advice on not getting upset?
- Have you ever missed me?

VERY IMPORTANT:
- Do you have a nice watch? Because I have never once had a birthday present from you, and I didn't mind before, but now I do a bit. (It wouldn't have to be a watch. Just a present of some sort.)

I know you can't answer because this is a

Better Letter, not a postable sort of letter,
but those are the questions I have thought of.

I hope you are well and very happy, and I'm
sorry I haven't thought about you very much
ever.

~~Love~~ from Pea xx

'Oh, *Pea*,' said Clover, reading it over her
shoulder. 'That's . . . It's . . . *Oh*. I'm sorry about
the watch. I didn't know it had made you feel like
that.'

'Neither did I, till I started writing,' said
Pea. 'And I'm glad your dad gave you a present,
honestly I am. Only it sort of reminded me mine
hasn't. Ever. I crossed out the *Love* because it made
me feel funny. Does it look mean, do you think?
I suppose it doesn't matter; it's not like he'll ever
read it.'

71

Tinkerbell chewed on a fingernail. 'What if he could?'

Pea giggled. 'Don't be daft. We haven't got his address. We don't know anything about him!'

But Clover was staring at Tinkerbell, her mouth falling open. 'No, Tink's right,' she said in a hushed voice. 'I can't post my letter to my dad. Tink can't post hers to Granny Duff. But your dad's still alive, somewhere. If we could find him, if we could track him down . . .'

'He really *could* give you a present for your birthday,' said Tinkerbell.

'For *every* birthday,' said Clover, wide-eyed. 'Just think. You could have a *dad*, Pea.'

CHAPTER 4

PETER RABBIT

Pea's insides felt like they were in the washing machine.

You could have a dad, Pea. Clover's words went round and round in her tummy, sloshing about. A dad, her own dad. Ewan McGregor: real, on their doorstep, piled up with birthday presents and saying *Sorry sorry sorry*. He'd have bright red hair, just like hers. His smile would be wide and warm. He'd call her Prudence, and she wouldn't mind.

(Pea's proper name was Prudence, but when she was small she had a lisp, and no one wants to go through life being called 'Pwudenthe'. She'd been Pea for so long that it felt like the real her – but she might make an exception for a real dad.)

Suddenly the washing machine stopped sloshing, with a thunk.

'But – wait – didn't Mum try to find him, years and years ago?' she said.

Tinkerbell frowned, and looked at Clover.

'You wouldn't remember: it was BT,' said Clover. (BT meant 'Before Tinkerbell'.) 'She did, yes. It was after The Flood. She had to get new passports, and reprinted birth certificates, and she got all worried about what would happen if she ever got poorly and couldn't look after us.'

Pea pictured it immediately: Mum suddenly taken ill, and Clover and Pea surviving as raggedy street urchins, forced to join a band of pickpockets, surviving by their wits. It sounded brilliant – until she remembered the Incredible Hulk slippers, and the mouldy smell after The Flood, and all the times when there hadn't been enough money to

74

go round. Adventures were all well and good, but really, a nice warm house with central heating and a fridge and a mum to fill it were better for every day.

'That's why we went back to Wales after Amsterdam, so she could see Granny Duff and make arrangements,' Clover continued. 'I don't think she got very far with finding him, though, Pea. She didn't have a computer at home; she had to go to one of those internet cafés. She said it was like playing hide-and-seek, only not fun. We started calling him Mean Old Mr McGregor like the farmer from *Peter Rabbit* – do you remember?'

Pea shook her head. She didn't remember anything like that. It didn't sound very fatherly.

In her head, the imaginary Ewan McGregor on the doorstep put down her big pile of presents and produced a shotgun, for shooting the bottoms off innocent carrot-eating rabbits.

'What if he was trying to hide?' said Pea, in a

small voice. 'Maybe he didn't want her to find him. Maybe—'

Wuffly's ears pricked up, and she scampered to the front door, barking as it opened, then slammed shut.

'Hello, my swans,' called Mum, in a gloomy voice. She shrugged off her coat, and flopped onto the sofa between Clover and Tinkerbell. 'Hope you're having a cheerfuller evening than me.'

'We're writing letters to dead people,' said Tinkerbell. 'And Pea's is—'

'Private,' said Pea, hastily folding up the letter to her dad and slipping it into her jeans pocket. She gave Clover and Tinkerbell a meaningful look, and they both nodded to show they understood it was a secret. Clover pressed her letter into Mum's hands as a distraction, and Pea started to explain about Dr Paget and Make-It-Better Letters while she read – but before she'd finished, Mum's mouth went crumply, and Pea broke off.

'I don't think Dr Paget meant it to make you

cry,' said Pea, mortified, as a tear plopped off Mum's nose.

'Oh no, Pea-pod, it's not her fault,' said Mum, ruffling Wuffly's ears fondly. 'I'm just feeling a bit wobbly today, that's all, with everything that's happened. And the film tonight turned out to be the sort with sad families being shouty, so we left before the end. Oh dear. I'm sorry, my chicks, I don't mean to be such a misery. It's lucky we've got three more birthdays coming up, isn't it? I need some nice surprises to look forward to.'

Mum looked at Clover's too-large watch, and gave the strap a stroke with her finger. Then she wrapped them all in one of her squeezy jasmine-perfume-smelling hugs, the sort that lasts a long time.

'Why didn't you ask her about Mean Old Mr McGregor?' whispered Tinkerbell, once Mum had gone to make herself a hot chocolate. 'Even if she never found out exactly where he is, she might know some clues.'

'Don't call him Mean Old Mr McGregor!' Pea whispered back.

'Oh!' gasped Clover, putting her hands to her lips. She jumped up, and pushed the door shut so no one could possibly overhear. 'You know how we haven't got Mum a birthday present yet?'

Pea and Tinkerbell both nodded heavily. Mum was notoriously difficult to buy presents for. She always said she didn't want them spending too much of their pocket money, and practical things were just as welcome as fun ones – but the year Clem had given her a set of bathroom scales and some minty scrub for getting dead skin off your feet remained fresh in the family memory.

'Listen: you want to find your dad, Pea,' said Clover, her eyes sparkling. 'Mum wants a surprise. And ever since Granny Duff died, she's been talking about how important families are. What if we found him, as our present to Mum? What if we could track him down, so you could both see him again?'

'You could invite him to your birthday party!' said Tinkerbell.

Pea could barely breathe.

Her imaginary Ewan McGregor lost his shotgun, and his pile of presents on the doorstep. Now he was popping out of a gigantic fake cake on the kitchen table, shouting 'Surprise!' in an American accent, and throwing confetti. Mum would cry, and call it the best birthday present ever. He'd move into a house on the other side of Queen's Park, and he'd pick her up from school every day and take her to the swanky café with the long wooden tables and the ginormous cakes, where she could have whatever she wanted, even if it spoiled her tea.

She was getting a bit ahead of herself with the planning, she knew, but still.

'That would be *amazing*,' she said softly.

'But what if he lives in America?' said Tinkerbell.

The swanky café dream began to unravel – but only for a moment.

Clover shook her head. 'Easy. You can talk to people on the other side of the world in two seconds with the internet. We'll track him down in no time. And we've got . . .' She counted off on her fingers. 'Twenty-one days till your and Mum's birthdays. Even if he's on the other side of the world, that's enough time for him to get on a plane. Besides, for all we know, he could be living just round the corner.'

Pea hugged her arms about herself, feeling warm all over.

Mum came back to drink her hot chocolate with them, and to snuggle up in front of a more cheerful film without any sad families being shouty – but Pea's letter to her dad felt loud in her pocket, as if it might jump out and shout their secret. In the end she took it upstairs, changed into her pyjamas, and perched on the end of her bed to re-read what she'd written.

I know you can't answer because this is a
Better Letter, not a postable sort of letter,
but those are the questions I have thought of.
I hope you are well and very happy, and I'm
sorry I haven't thought about you very much ever.

~~Love~~ from Pea xx

It was only a letter, not a postable letter even
– but perhaps that didn't matter. Perhaps she'd
get to ask him her questions herself, face to face,
after all.

She tucked the letter away in her bedside drawer,
and went to sleep with a smile on her face.

Pea was woken up the next morning by a yell of
'*Travello acrosso roomo!*' When she opened one eye,
she was greeted by the sight of Wuffly's hairy
nose a millimetre from her own – and Tinkerbell,

wearing a bow tie and a twirly moustache drawn on with Clover's eyeliner pencil.

'*Levitatus Wuffliato!*' yelled Tinkerbell, brandishing her felt-tip wand at Wuffly.

Wuffly licked Pea's nose, and showed no sign of Levitatusing.

'Get off, silly dog,' said Pea, pushing her away as she sat up. 'What *are* you doing?'

'Training Wuffly to be my magician's assistant,' said Tinkerbell crossly, as if it were obvious. 'And trying to learn some new tricks. I thought if I could learn how to make a dog move from one side of the room to the other, then by your birthday I might be able to make a *person* move from one side of the planet to the other. Only she won't stay still long enough for me to practise properly. It doesn't matter, though. We probably won't need magic anyway.'

Pea sat patiently in bed, watching Tinkerbell's efforts to make Wuffly teleport.

Once the clock had ticked around to nine, they woke Clover up.

'It's still far too early for a Sunday,' she said disgustedly. 'I am a teenager, you know. It's exhausting – just you wait.'

Clover pulled the duvet over her face – but they came back with a tray of toast with peanut butter, tea and orange juice, and she was placated. They sat on the end of her bed to plan their dad-finding campaign. Tinkerbell had appointed herself Campaign Manager. She had brought *My First Atlas* with her (the perfect-sized book for hiding secret plans), with a thick wodge of lined paper tucked inside. The front page had

OPERASHUN: PETER RABBIT

written across it.

'Opera-what?' said Pea.

'Operation,' said Tinkerbell, scowling when Pea took the pen and corrected her spelling.

'What's the Peter Rabbit bit for?' asked Clover, sipping her orange juice.

83

Tinkerbell rolled her eyes. 'Duh! It's our secret codename for Pea's dad. Because of Mean Old Mr McGregor? And so Mum won't realize what our secret plan is. If we want to have a meeting to do plotting, or have found an important thing out, we can say, "I need to talk to you about Peter Rabbit," or "Oh look, there's Peter Rabbit" – and she won't suspect a thing.'

'I think she might suspect *something*,' said Pea.

'But not the *secret* thing,' said Tinkerbell. 'Trust me, I'm better than you at secret plans.'

That much was probably true, so Pea didn't argue.

'Now,' Tinkerbell continued, 'I've made a list of everything we know about Peter Rabbit, and that way we'll know where to start looking.'

Greece
America
Ginger (magically curly?) hair/big chin

84

It was a rather short list. Pea added:

The Beatles

underneath.

'Because I'm named after a Beatles song. I think it must have been his favourite.'

The song was called *Dear Prudence*. It had jangly guitars, and the words were all about a little girl going to a playground, as far as Pea could tell; if Tinkerbell hadn't insisted on singing 'Dear Pwudenthe' along to it whenever Mum put it on, it would've been one of her favourites. Pea had always imagined Ewan McGregor strumming on a guitar and crooning it at Mum's bedside, while her baby-sized self lay sleeping in a hospital cot, somewhere hot and sunny. If she'd only just been born, it couldn't possibly be a memory, really – but it felt true.

'That doesn't help,' said Tinkerbell. 'Everyone likes The Beatles.'

'Greece is the obvious place to start,' said

Clover. 'Since that's where Mum last saw him.'

'On a Greek island,' corrected Pea.

Tinkerbell flipped through *My First Atlas* until she found the Mediterranean. 'There are loads of them!' she said, disgusted. 'I thought we could go there and ask people if they remembered Mum – but that would take *for ever.*'

She flipped through her pages, pulled out a drawing of a plane, and scrumpled it up. 'That makes *America* no good as a clue either,' she grumbled. 'Now we're looking for a man with magic ginger hair and a big chin. This is impossible already.'

'Red hair,' said Pea quietly. 'Red, not ginger. It's more polite.'

Clover grabbed the last piece of toast and hopped out of bed. 'You're both ignoring the biggest clue of all. Come on, we'll have to be quick.'

They followed her downstairs, into Mum's study. There was paper everywhere: the pages of *Mermaid Girls 4: Waterfall Magic*, with squiggles in blue pencil where a spelling mistake had crept in, or a comma was supposed to be a full stop, and had to be fixed before the book went off to be properly printed. Next to those were more scribbly notes about book five. And when they turned on Mum's computer, there was a picture of Tenby beach as a background, and lots of little icons – for email, for the internet, and so on.

Among them was one that looked like a page, called 'New Book Ideas'.

Pea longed to click on it. Her finger hovered over the mouse – but they could hear footsteps creaking down the stairs.

'If Mum comes in we'll pretend we're doing homework,' hissed Tinkerbell.

The footsteps shuffled straight past. There was the sound of cupboards opening and closing in the kitchen. The smell of fresh brewing coffee and toast wafted in.

Tinkerbell was stationed at the door, as a guard,

while Clover typed, quickly but carefully so the keyboard didn't clatter.

'See? We just need to look up *Ewan McGregor*. The internet's going to do all the hard detective stuff for us,' she said.

But it turned out that putting *Ewan McGregor* into Google brought up millions of results.

'Whoa,' breathed Tinkerbell. 'Your dad's even more famous than Mum!'

Clover scrolled through page after page of pictures of a handsome actor with blue eyes and a cheeky grin, as if he was having a private joke with the person taking the photo. In some of the pictures his hair was definitely reddish, and when he had a beard his chin looked fairly big.

'But he can't possibly be my dad,' said Pea. 'Look – he's Scottish, not American. Besides, by the time Mum met *my* Ewan McGregor, this one was busy being a Jedi in *Star Wars*.'

'Maybe that's why he ran away – to be a Jedi?'

said Tinkerbell – but even she didn't sound as if she believed it.

Clover sighed. 'It's a shame he's not the right Ewan McGregor. He's got a nice face. And he'd be ever so useful for getting me an acting job in a film, once I've stopped being Alice.'

Pea nudged Clover out of the chair, and tried typing in *other Ewan McGregors* and *Ewan McGregors who aren't famous*, but it was hopeless. Finding out more about Ewan McGregor the handsome Scottish actor was easy. Finding out about a different one was next to impossible.

If he'd been planning to hide from her, Pea thought, their Peter Rabbit couldn't have picked a better name.

'I know,' said Tinkerbell, pushing Pea's shoulder till she let her sit. 'We could put in *ginger* – sorry, *red – hair* and *Beatles* together. That would—'

'What *are* you lot doing?' said Mum.

Pea squeaked. Tinkerbell had completely forgotten to guard the door, and now Mum was standing right there, with a mug of coffee in one hand.

'Nothing!' yelped Clover, clicking the little 'x' so the screen full of Ewan McGregors vanished, and the wallpaper of Tenby beach reappeared.

Mum frowned. 'Oh dear. I wasn't worried before, but now I might be. You know I don't like you coming in here without asking.'

Pea and Clover exchanged confused looks. They came into the study to do homework or email Clem all the time; she'd never minded it before.

Mum peered closer at the screen, then her face darkened. 'You didn't *read* anything, did you?' she said, in an unusually severe voice.

All three sisters shook their heads.

'Pea?'

Pea's eyes had drifted back to the screen; to the 'New Book Ideas' file, sitting there temptingly.

She shook her head again, very fast. 'I wanted to look at the new book, but I didn't. Really, truly.'

'She didn't read a thing,' said Clover. 'None of us did.'

Mum looked searchingly at Pea. 'Glad to hear it. Keep it that way. Although I'm still not—'

Suddenly her suspicious expression vanished, to be replaced with a soft smile. 'Oh, my fluffy ducks! How daft am I? You're looking online for ideas for my birthday present, aren't you?'

Pea looked shiftily at Clover, then at Tinkerbell. It was *sort* of true. She shuffled her shoulders in a half-yes, but Mum threw up her hands.

'Sorry, sorry, I should know better at birthday time! So long as you completely promise to keep your noses out of my writing, then go ahead! Be secretive! Lie! Fib till your lips go blue!' And she hurried away.

'Brilliant!' said Tinkerbell. 'Now if she wonders what we're up to while we're looking for Peter Rabbit, we can say it's a birthday-present thing.'

Pea didn't think it was all that brilliant; not when Ewan McGregor was going to be so much harder to find than she'd hoped. And not when Mum was being so secretive about her new book.

I can't write about mermaids for ever, Mum had told the *London Now* journalist. And her 'inspirational' children *were* growing up . . .

Had Mum given up on the three mermaid girls already? Were her 'New Book Ideas' all for adults?

Not that there was anything wrong with grown-up books, exactly – Pea was sure they'd be very good; Mum was a brilliant writer, after all – but as far as she could tell they were mostly about wars, deaths, or ladies who spent all day long thinking about some hairy man they wanted to kiss. Mum's books would suddenly have a big shoe on the front cover, instead of sparkles and mermaids. However mature and sophisticated she was becoming, Pea didn't know anything about shoes, or wanting to kiss hairy men. Mum wouldn't want her help with any of it.

'Chin up,' said Tinkerbell, giving Pea a wonky

smile. (She'd rubbed her hand across her face, and now all that was left of her twirly eyeliner moustache was one smeary curl.) 'I'll find the real Peter Rabbit for you in no time.' She gave her felt-pen wand a flourish.

'I think it might take more than a magic trick,' said Clover. 'We need the police, really. Or a private detective. Expensive.'

'We can do detecting! Dig for clues, interview witnesses . . . Ooh, we should interrogate Mum!' Tinkerbell beamed. 'It's almost always someone in the family who dunnit, on TV.'

'That's murders, Tink,' said Clover. 'He hasn't been murdered.'

'No, he definitely hasn't!' said Pea hotly.

'And you can't interrogate Mum, not if it's going to be a birthday surprise,' added Clover. 'If you suddenly ask hundreds of questions about him, she'll get suspicious. I'm sorry, Pea. I don't think this is going to work.'

But Pea shook her head firmly.

'No I'm not giving up. Not when we've only just started.'

It wouldn't matter if Mum didn't need her help with the new book; not if Pea was busy with her dad.

Besides, it was better this way; if he'd been easy to find, it wouldn't be anywhere near as exciting. Her imaginary Ewan McGregor reappeared on the doorstep – with a handsome face, a red-tinged beard, and a private grin of admiration for his clever detective daughter.

Now all she had to do was find him.

CHAPTER
5

DETECTIVE
INSPECTOR PEA

Pea went to school on Monday morning filled with
Peter Rabbit-hunting determination. Her first stop
was the school library, before lessons had even
begun.

'You're keen, Pea,' said Miss Pond, yawning as
she fumbled for her keys. 'Looking for more sad
death books, are we?'

Pea shook her head. 'Detectives, please. It's
research for a sort of project.'

If she was going to dig for clues, she needed

expert guidance. Miss Pond gave her *Ruby Redfort*, and *Young Sherlock Holmes*.

Pea started on Ruby at once, and got told off in Mr Ellis's English class for reading it under the desk while Shruti did an oral presentation about 'Musical Instruments from Around the World'. By lunch time, she couldn't wait to get back to it. As usual, she ate packed lunch with Bethany, Molly and Eloise. Eloise put her headphones in and munched away, nodding her head to the music. Molly listened politely as Bethany described her new 1-Click Dream poster in loving detail, while Pea unwrapped her sandwiches one-handed, and turned to the next page with crumby fingers.

'Good book?' asked Molly eventually, sounding slightly desperate to stop talking about swooshy hair.

Pea opened her mouth, then shut it again. Until they'd definitely found him, she didn't want to let on to her friends about Operation Peter Rabbit. She especially didn't want to say anything in front of Molly. Molly's dad used to come to watch the Kensal Rise Kites matches, even after Molly had stopped playing for the team. He'd always seemed kind, and funny, but Molly's parents were recently 'estranged', which meant that her dad had moved out and now Molly only saw him at weekends. Acting Deputy Head Mrs King had taken Pea and Bethany aside after assembly one day, and asked them to be extra-kind to her about it. Pea had understood at once. She'd only been eight when Clem had first moved out of their flat in Tenby, but she remembered how strange it had felt not to see his shoes by the front door or his blue dressing gown on its hook. It would be mean to rub in the fact that Pea's real dad was about to reappear in her life, just as Molly's had left.

'Very good, thanks,' she mumbled.

It was, too – though she wasn't sure how useful it would be for Operation Peter Rabbit, unless her dad suddenly started leaving her codes to crack and clues to solve.

Luckily, by the time they got home from school Tinkerbell's own secret plan was well underway. She was sitting at the kitchen table, surrounded by mountainous piles of books and sheets of paper, a look of gleeful pride on her face.

'What's all this?' asked Clover, eyeing her warily.

'Just play along,' hissed Tinkerbell. Then she sat up and yelled, 'Mum! Muuu-uum! We need you in the kitchen!'

The sound of rapid typing stopped abruptly.

'I hope you've got a broken limb of some kind, Tink,' shouted Mum, poking her head out of the study. 'The sign on this door expressly says I'm not to be disturbed unless there are endangered limbs!'

Pea sighed. The new book for grown-ups was obviously going well; Mum loved being interrupt-ed when she was stuck.

'Though I suppose I'd better get dinner started if we're . . . Oh my. I knew you were going to the library on the way home from school, but I didn't think you were going to bring *all* their books home. What are these for?' Curious, Mum came into the kitchen and picked up a book from the pile. '*Greece through the Ages? Ancient Greece?*'

'Ohhh,' murmured Pea, catching Clover's eye and understanding at once.

'It's for a school project,' said Tinkerbell. 'My group got Greece,' she added.

'I can see that,' said Mum.

'Wait, I've just remembered. Didn't you use to live on a Greek island, Mum?'

Clover's voice sounded slightly unnatural, but Mum didn't notice. She smiled, and stroked Pea's ponytail.

'You know I did, flower – you did too. That's where Pea was born, a little island called Cephalonia. And before that I lived on Crete. But I won't be any use for a project, Tink. I expect they want you to write about Greek gods and myths, not sunny beaches full of tourists.'

'No,' said Clover swiftly. 'Other people are

doing that part of the project. Tink's part is about what Greece is like to live in now. Isn't it?'

Tinkerbell nodded, a lot.

With a sideways glance at Clover, Mum sat down. 'Oh, it was a long time ago, my starling. What do you want to know?'

Pea felt a thrill run down her spine. This was it. All they had to do was ask the right questions, and Mum might let slip the clue that would lead them directly to their Peter Rabbit.

Tinkerbell picked up her pen, as if about to take notes. 'Tell me absolutely everything about Cephalonia,' she said.

Mum's face melted into a dreamy smile, and she tilted her head to one side. 'Oh, it was beautiful. The sea so blue, and always sparkling in the sun or twinkling in the moonlight. There's a beach, a famous one, with a colony of sea turtles. Fishing boats in the harbour. Olives, and cheese – and so many people. There was a book around that time, and then a film of the book, about a soldier who fell in love with a Greek girl on the island. People came from all over the world, hoping they might fall in love too.'

Pea glanced at Clover. It was the perfect opportunity.

'And did you fall in love there too, Mum?' she asked, in a breathless whisper.

Mum's dreamy smile faded for a second, then came back even stronger. 'Of course I did, darling! I told you, that's where you were born. I'll never forget the moment they put you into my arms. The best birthday present imaginable.'

'Yes, but—' said Pea.

'Crete's beautiful too,' said Mum quickly, standing up and poking through the fridge. Then she launched into a long description of famous archaeological sites on Crete, which had mermaid carvings on and which had probably inspired the *Mermaid Girls* books – all while taking things out of the fridge for dinner, then absent-mindedly putting them back again.

Then the phone rang in the hallway.

'Oh! That'll be the Dreaditor!' said Mum.

Usually when Mum's Dreaded Editor called, she went pale, and sometimes hid under a cushion until it went to voicemail. But this time she positively sprinted towards the phone, and disappeared into the study at top speed.

'That's weird,' said Tinkerbell.

'Very weird,' agreed Clover, 'unless she really does want to have lettuce and tomato ketchup for dinner.' She put them back in the fridge with a frown. 'Did you notice – when she started talking it was like she didn't want to look anyone in the eye? It was almost as if she was . . .'

Lying, Pea thought. Or keeping something secret, anyway.

'At least we know which Greek island it was now,' said Tinkerbell. 'That's got to be a useful clue, right?'

Pea hoped so. She waited patiently until Mum started cooking dinner – but when she went to look up *Cephalonia* + *Ewan McGregor* on the computer, she found she couldn't open the study door.

'Oh no you don't!' called Mum from the kitchen when she heard Pea waggling the handle. She held up her key-ring and jingled it triumphantly. As well as the front- and back-door keys, and the knotty key-ring Tinkerbell had made in after-school club, there was now a shiny golden key dangling from the metal loop.

'It's *locked*?'

'Out of bounds for everyone who isn't me – sorry!'

Then she went back to chopping onions, as if a locked study was perfectly unmysterious.

That was that, then, Pea thought sadly: Mum definitely didn't want her help with the new book. And it was most inconvenient for digging for Cephalonian clues.

Clover was no help. Pea found her shut inside her wardrobe, so she could 'authentically appreciate the fearful darkness of Alice's fall down the rabbit-hole'.

'Sorry, Pea, I have to be left alone in here for at least an hour,' she said in a muffled voice, 'or Marko says I won't experience the bleak reality of solitude. Apparently Alices need that.'

Pea and Tinkerbell flicked through all the Greece books, but none of them even mentioned Cephalonia.

They sat on the new red sofa and pored over the family albums again, in case just one photograph of Ewan McGregor might have somehow escaped The Flood. They were still there, Pea feeling rather sorry for herself, when Noelle came back from her English lesson.

'*Bonjour, le Drip!*' yelled Tinkerbell. 'I've decided not to do a project about Greece after all. Can you take all these back to the library for me tomorrow?'

'Tink!' said Pea, elbowing her. 'Don't be cheeky.'

'Cheeky,' murmured Noelle, rolling the word around in her mouth. 'What is *cheeky*?'

'It's when you have big puffy cheeks, like a

squirrel eating nuts,' said Tinkerbell, running away before she could be told off.

Pea explained that it had nothing to do with squirrels, and eventually fetched the dictionary.

'*Ah, je comprends. Insolent, coquine,*' said Noelle huskily. She blew her nose, then, seeing the open photograph albums, offered Pea a tissue too. 'If you are unhappy for the grandmother Duff?'

'Oh, no thank you, I'm all right. And it's not that exactly,' said Pea, frowning. 'I miss my dad, I think. If you can miss things you can't remember, or a thing you never had. I don't know how to look up the word for that.'

Pea could sense Noelle's incomprehension through her hair curtains, even though she couldn't really see her face.

'Sorry, it's quite confusing for me too. How was your lesson?'

Noelle managed a wan smile. 'My teacher, Tansy, she is telling me to write letters, like your Dr Paget. I am writing to my family in English, and she is changing the words if I am bad. I learn very good. But now I have the homesick again.'

Pea nodded fervently. *That* was the word. Here she was, in her own front room – but somehow she had the homesick too.

'Marko is *so* clever,' Clover declared as they waited for the bus the next day. 'Being in the wardrobe yesterday gave me a whole new perspective on the role. I think my Alice is going to be a very tragical, damaged soul. With broken ankles, from falling so far. Oh, hang on, I have to start today's visualization exercise now. *Oh heavens, what is that fearful wheeled monster!*'

Marko's task for the day was for Clover to imagine herself as a girl from 1865, who had fallen down a time/rabbit-hole to now. Pea didn't mind explaining mobile phones and women wearing trousers at first, but Alice-Clover from 1865 proved trying company, and was no help at all when Pea tried – with no success – to use the library computers to look up Ewan McGregors on Cephalonia.

When she got home, Pea went straight up the stairs to her little attic room to escape all the '*Ah me, how strange this place is!*' sighing.

She wanted to write; not the rest of the Mashed Potato Poisoning story about Sky, or any more M & S mermaid ideas. She would start a new Amy story with shoes and kissing, which would prove to Mum that she was ready to help with her new book. The Amy stories didn't have any spare hairy men for her to kiss so far, unfortunately; really Batthew the Bat was the only candidate – but perhaps Batthew could turn out to be under an enchantment, like the Frog Prince? Pea wasn't sure she wanted to write a kissing scene between Amy and a bat, and pondered an alternative version with a spell that could be broken with a nice friendly hug while she looked for her rainbow notebook.

But it wasn't in its usual spot, on her desk. It wasn't in her school bag. She searched and searched, but she couldn't find it anywhere.

It was no use asking Mum if she'd seen it: she could hear typing from behind the study door, and there was a Post-it note stuck to it:

DANGER!
SHARK-INFESTED STUDY
KEEP OUT OR YOU WILL
BE CHOMPED

Noelle shook her hair curtains solemnly when Pea tapped on her door to ask if she'd seen it.

'*Non*,' she said, her voice soft. 'Today I clean bedrooms, it is true: I see many things – but I do not see book of rainbows.'

When Tinkerbell went next door for another puppy-training session, Pea followed, to see if she'd accidentally left it there.

Sam One hadn't seen the rainbow notebook

either, but Pea stayed for lemon squash and a biscuit. She meant to tell him all about the new Amy story idea, with Batthew, and hugging, but before she knew it, she was telling him all about Clover's watch, and Operation Peter Rabbit – far away from Sam Two (who was very good at keeping her own secrets, but blabby with other people's).

'. . . And I know it's a bit silly, really, to think we could find him in time for my birthday. But I do want to try. Everyone else has got a dad – why can't I?'

Sam One frowned beneath his floppy fringe.

Pea's hands flew to her lips. 'I'm so sorry! I didn't mean . . . I wasn't . . .'

'Don't go all weird, I was only thinking,' said Sam One. 'I've got two parents – that's more than lots of people. And I have got a dad, sort of. I mean, we know who he is. He's called Malcolm. My mums have known him for years; they were friends at university, and when they wanted to have some babies they asked him to be the donor. But we don't call him Dad, and he doesn't give us presents.

It would be a bit funny if he did, I think. He's just a stranger who happened to help make us exist.'

Pea sat quietly. That was all Ewan McGregor was, once you took away the made-up parts about him being a pirate.

'That doesn't mean you shouldn't look for yours, though,' said Sam One, scratching his nose. 'If I didn't know there was a Malcolm, I'd probably want to find out about him. But you should be prepared for yours to turn out to be old and have a moustache, because that can happen.'

That night, Pea tried reading her Young Sherlock Holmes book. He seemed very clever, but people did keep arriving on his doorstep with telltale red mud on their boots or distinctive crinkles in their ears, which felt a little like cheating when all Pea had to go on was the possibility of magic red hair and a fondness for Beatles songs. Her rainbow notebook was still missing, but notepaper felt more appropriate for a letter anyway, even one she'd never send.

Dear Ewan McGregor,
I don't want you to think I am giving up or
anything, but detecting is quite difficult
without any clues at all. If we only knew you
liked to smoke Russian cigarettes or had a
tattoo, we would have a much better chance.

I suppose I'm the best clue we've got. I
always thought I was like Mum because we
both love writing. but maybe that's only
because I don't know you. I am better at
being on time than Mum is, and I worry about
things more, and I am better at cooking pasta
because I use the timer and she always leaves
it too long so it's floppy. Are you those things
too?

If you were. I could probably work out
loads about where you might be now by being
Sherlock Holmes-ish. The pasta thing means you
could be a chef? But anyone can make pasta if
they use the timer. Being on time could make you
a train driver or a police officer – or any job,

really. I don't think worrying a lot qualifies you for anything. I hope you're something brilliant and amazing, like a rock climber who goes up mountains and rescues people, or a doctor who keeps tiny babies alive. I wouldn't mind you going off to do that instead of being my dad. But if you suddenly gave all that up and came here, it would be brilliant, and I'm pretty sure we'd forget all about you being a rubbish dad up till now quite quickly.

I actually would like a watch for a birthday present, as well.

I'm glad this is only a Better Letter. I would be quite embarrassed if you ever actually read it.

Love from Pea xx

CHAPTER

6

M & S

Pea's head was still full of imaginary dads on doorsteps, but on Wednesday morning the conversation at breakfast was all birthdays.

'So, Clem's going to arrive on Friday night, Tink,' Mum said, yawning as she spread butter on her toast. 'Cliff and Joe and all the little cousins can't make it, but they sent their love.'

'Did they send presents as well?' asked Tinkerbell.

Mum ignored this. 'And the Amazing Sylvester's booked for three o'clock on Saturday.'

'Will he saw Blonde Annabel in half?'

'Doubtful,' said Mum.

'Can he make me turn invisible?'

'Let's hope so, eh?'

'Must I be a mouse, with ears?' whispered Noelle.

Mum shook her head. 'No, no costumes for this party. A magician, not-quite-croquet in the garden, and some DVDs for afterwards. All right with everyone? Good. Now, Pea: I need to know if I'm getting extra tickets for Clover's play, or booking somewhere. Have you decided what you'd like for your party yet?'

Pea stifled a secret smile. 'Not exactly.'

'I think a Peter Rabbit theme would be good, don't you?' squeaked Clover, giving Pea a smirky wink. (Marko had instructed her to spend all day imagining herself shrinking every time she had anything to drink. Her morning cup of tea had already rendered her almost inaudible.)

'Really?' said Mum. 'Isn't that a bit childish for you, Pea-nut? Though I suppose you've already got the fluffy bunny ears. We could have carrot cake . . .'

'No, she didn't mean – I don't want—' said Pea, blushing. She was far too M & S for a Peter Rabbit party: surely Mum understood that?

'Who is Rabbit?' whispered Noelle from behind her hair.

Mum got distracted into a long explanation of Beatrix Potter characters, and Pea could eat her cereal in peace. But as she pulled on her coat to catch the bus to school, Mum called after her, 'Party ideas, Pea! You need to choose this week. Don't forget!'

Pea was stuck. The party theme was already fixed: her dad, jumping out of a cake. But she couldn't tell Mum that; not without ruining her surprise birthday reunion.

Of course, it was always possible he'd be busy cooking pasta or rescuing people that weekend. She supposed it made sense to have a back-up plan.

Her school friends were brimming with suggestions.

'We'll help you think of the *perfect* party,' said Bethany on the way to English. 'What about a 1-Click Dream theme? With singing, and—'

'It's Pea's birthday, not yours,' said Molly. 'We should make a list of everyone's ideas.'

It was difficult to scribble down plans under the piercing blue gaze of Mr Ellis, especially after he'd caught Pea reading on Monday, but she sneaked a piece of paper under the desk, and jotted them down in between underlining pre-positions.

BIRTHDAY PLANS

Dress-up-as-a-boy-band party (or a girl band, if you want to be a girl band)
Karaoke party
Re-enacting a video from a band that you like and getting your mum or someone to record it and put it on YouTube

Something simple with a nice cake
Makeovers
Cinema
Bowling
Pizza (with us doing our own toppings)
Going out for pizza
Staying in for pizza
Mermaids

'Well?' said Bethany as they left Mr Ellis's classroom.

'Um,' said Pea.

She meant: *Which one would Ewan McGregor like best?* It might be the first time they met. It had to be something that would make him proud of his mature, sophisticated daughter. It had to be perfect.

'Makeovers would be best,' said Bethany confidently. 'Shruti Cox-Patel had a mini beautifying spa day for hers. It was like going to the hairdresser's, only longer.'

'Really?' Pea crinkled up her nose.

Mum took her to the hairdresser's every three months or so, for a trim. She usually took a book to make it go quicker. The idea that it might be a birthday treat was baffling.

Molly tucked her arm comfortingly through Pea's. 'Don't panic, Pea, I bet Eloise has loads of ideas.'

Eloise's parents had a catering company that made fancy food for weddings, and for people in offices who really liked triangular sandwiches.

'Yeah, they do birthdays sometimes,' said Eloise at lunch time, once she'd taken out her headphones. 'Let me think. Medieval Banquet – that's where your plate is made out of bread, and they roast a whole pig with its head still on.'

'I don't want that,' said Pea at once.

'Or there's Hawaiian Dream: pineapples scooped out with other fruit put inside them, and all the servers wear grass skirts and bras made out of coconuts.'

'Sounds cold,' Molly commented.

'I don't like coconut,' said Pea. 'It tastes like sunscreen. I'm sure it would be nice for someone else's party, but it doesn't sound very me-ish.'

Eloise chewed the inside of her cheek. 'Hmm, something you-ish . . . Don't think they've ever done a mermaid one, but I suppose you could. Blue drinks, bowls of crispy seaweed . . .'

'Mermaids? Ugh,' said Bethany, rolling her eyes.

Pea hesitated. Was it mature and sophisticated to have a mermaid party? Or was a mermaid party, perhaps, a little bit like a Peter Rabbit party?

'Yeah, ugh,' she said, nodding along uncomfortably. 'No mermaids. Yuck to mermaids.'

Molly blinked at her in surprise from behind her black-framed glasses.

119

'Fine – only trying to help,' said Eloise, crossly shuffling her shoulders and popping the middle button of her school blouse. (Eloise had always been quite busty compared to the other girls in Pea's class, but she seemed especially so today. Pea caught a glimpse of her bra through the gap in her blouse: white, with a faint pink rose pattern. How impossible life was, she thought, when there were busty girls with pink roses on their bras in her class, and mini beautifying spa days, while Pea – if she were being absolutely honest – would actually quite like to have a birthday party to do with mermaids.)

'Um,' said Pea. 'I'll think about it.'

That evening, Mum went off to her life-drawing class with Klaudia without asking about birthday decisions, much to Pea's relief.

Noelle was meant to be looking after them while they all did homework, but she had homework of her own to finish for Tansy – a letter to her father in English – and kept nudging Pea's elbow to ask her in a whisper if 'I am terrible unhappy with the homesick' and 'I not like it here' were correct.

Pea found it quite demoralizing.

'Maybe doing something French would help you feel less homesick? You could teach me how to cook something for dinner. What's traditional where you come from?'

Noelle gave a sigh. '*Crêpes, peut-être? Galettes? Parce que— Ah, en anglais . . .*'

'Oh! We have *crêpes* here too – though we usually call them pancakes.'

Pea had hoped for omelettes or perhaps apple tart, but pancakes was even better.

Noelle scribbled down a list of ingredients in her loopy handwriting. Then, to Pea's surprise, she yawned and went to lie down in her bedroom.

At first it was alarming, being left in charge of cooking crêpes for four people for dinner – but what could be more mature and sophisticated than that? Noelle obviously thought she could manage.

As she whisked the eggs and milk into the flour, Pea felt a surge of confidence. She could have a French food party for her birthday: a banquet, cooked by hand. She drew the line at garlicky snails, but there would be hot baguettes, and fizzy apple juice, like cider. Everyone would stand in the kitchen and coo at her remarkable crêpe-tossing skills.

'She's a natural,' they would say.

'Just like her dad!' a voice would boom from the doorstep – and there he'd be: Ewan McGregor, dressed in a stripy top and a beret, ringing a bicycle bell.

(He was American, not French – and even Noelle had never worn a beret or ridden a bicycle – but still, it looked right in her head.)

Pea grated cheese and chopped up mushrooms, for savoury ones; cut up a lemon for the ones with sugar. She heated up the frying pan. She poured in a dribble of batter, and watched it spread out into a pancake-shape.

But when she tried to flip it over, it stuck to the

pan. She tried digging under it with a knife, but it turned into a pale thick clump.

Her next try went clumpy too.

'Ow!' Pea yelped, burning her fingertips as she tried to scoop batter back into the big hole that appeared in the middle of the third. By the time she'd run her fingers under the cold tap, the batter had turned black.

The fourth one began to look quite a lot like a pancake, all lacy round the edges – but when Pea jerked the pan to flip it over, it landed on the edge of the cooker, then slithered onto the floor.

Wuffly gobbled it up at once.

Pea tried adding cheese and mushrooms to the pan first, in case that helped. But the cheese glued itself to the pan, so when she poured batter over the top it got even more stuck than before.

The next attempt was so burned that even Wuffly wouldn't eat it.

'What's that horrible smell?' squeaked Clover, tiptoeing

into the kitchen. 'Oh, it's you. You shouldn't be left to cook pancakes by yourself, you're too young.'

'I think Le Drip should take over,' said Tinkerbell, eating Pea's grated cheese. 'Urgently.'

Pea couldn't disagree.

Noelle's crêpes turned out perfectly. Pea ate hers with her unsophisticated sore fingers, as all thoughts of French banquets and berets sank.

Dear Ewan McGregor,
I think you must definitely be a rock climber, not a chef.

What sort of birthday party do you think I should have?

I could do something outdoorsy. Maybe we could do rock climbing, and then, if I fell off, you could rescue me? That would be a good way for us to meet. But then, if I had a rock-climbing party and you turned out not to be a rescue man, I might fall off and die, and that would be a terrible birthday.

Is rock climbing mature and sophisticated?
I don't think London has many rocks anyway.
By the way, I have been thinking that instead of a watch you could buy me a bra with pink roses on. I know you are a boy and you might be embarrassed buying a girl's thing, but that is part of parenthood and you have been a bit lazy so far, so tough.

Love from Pea xx

Clover's task for Marko on Thursday was to imagine herself growing ever larger 'to experience a world where everyone else seems tiny and insignificant' – which mostly seemed to involve being loud, and taking up half of Pea's seat on the bus.

School didn't do much to cheer Pea up. She'd forgotten her PE kit and had to borrow a spare one that smelled of onions. And at lunch, the topic of birthday parties would not go away. Pea had reached such a state of confusion about what was suitably M & S that she barely dared to offer an opinion, even on what flavour of cake she should have at her own party.

'There doesn't need to be a stupid theme, anyway,' said Bethany. 'What about a sleepover?'

'Yes!' Pea said. 'A sleepover. That's what I want.' It would do. She could copy Clover's, so she wouldn't get anything too wrong. The 'special surprise guest' was the important part; she didn't really care about the rest.

Molly looked anxious. Eloise nodded approvingly (although she'd put her headphones back in, so she might have been nodding to the music really).

Bethany beamed. 'Yay! Who's coming? We're all invited, aren't we?'

'Of course! It'll be us four. And my friend Sam from next door.'

Molly wrinkled her nose. 'I thought you didn't like her?'

'No, not Sam Two. *Sam*. Sam the boy,' said Pea.

'He can't come to a sleepover party!' said Bethany, collapsing with laughter.

'Why not?'

'Because he's a boy, stupid!'

Pea looked at Molly for support, but Molly shook her head. 'He really can't,' she said gravely. 'Boys don't ever have sleepovers with girls, it's not allowed. Or . . . well, even if it's allowed, it's definitely not *usual*.'

'It's not really usual to have a boy as a friend anyway, Pea,' said Bethany, patting her arm as if offering helpful advice.

'You've got loads of boys on your bedroom walls,' said Pea.

'Not the same.'

'But he's nice! I mean, he's loads nicer than his sister is. We're really good friends. I can't *not* invite him to my birthday party.'

'Well, if a *boy* is coming,' said Bethany, making a sick noise when she said *boy*, 'then I'm not.'

Molly and Eloise didn't say anything – but they didn't promise to come, either.

'Um,' said Pea. 'Maybe I won't have a sleepover, then . . . Or,' she went on quickly as Bethany's face darkened, 'I might, still? I could not invite Sam, I suppose, if . . . um . . . I'll talk to my mum tonight.' She mumbled something about having to change her library book, then fled. But on her way out at the end of lunch break, she bumped into Molly, lingering outside and fiddling with her stripy brown and yellow tie.

'You know your sleepover party? Will it be on a Saturday? Only I stay at my dad's every other Saturday, and . . . Please, it's not that I don't want to come, only he gets upset, and if I don't go, Mum will say it's because I don't want to see him, and—'

Molly broke off with a sniff. 'Life's all a bit difficult at the moment.'

Pea – who felt that this was a very grown-up-seeming thing to have to manage – walked with her to the girls' toilets, so she could wash her face.

'I'll think of something, I promise,' Pea told her.

Molly gave her a grateful wobbly smile – but Pea had no idea what to do.

On the bus, Clover confessed that she'd 'quite like to stay larger than everyone for ever, if it was allowed'.

But Pea had begun to feel as if *she* was the one full of EAT ME cake, transforming into a whole new person – one she did not like at all.

She'd pretended to not like mermaids. She'd thought about bras, in a hopeful sort of way. She was even seriously considering not inviting Sam One to her party – when he was the only friend she'd been able to tell about Operation Peter Rabbit. He wouldn't like having his hair put in plaits, or giggling, or people mentioning bras; if it was that sort of party he might prefer not to come. But if it was a party he wasn't welcome at, Pea wasn't sure she wanted to, either – and she hated the idea of poor Molly being left out every bit as much.

The instant they got home, Pea went to the study. The Post-it on the door had a drawing of a skull and crossbones:

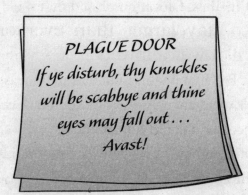

PLAGUE DOOR
If ye disturb, thy knuckles will be scabbye and thine eyes may fall out . . .
Avast!

Pea knocked anyway, again and again, until Mum appeared.

'What?' she said fiercely, her hair knotted up in

two pencils and her Special Writing Mug clutched in one hand.

'I know you're very busy writing your New Book, but I need to talk to you,' Pea began – quickly so Mum couldn't shut the door, 'and I sort of need some help because I know I should want to be bigger, not tiny-small – but I'd really rather stay the same because I think probably friends are more important than swooshy hair and bras – only now it's all gone complicated and – and—'

Mum's fierce look turned soft and smiley before Pea could accidentally blurt out anything to do with imaginary dads on the doorstep.

'Oh, come in, my poor funny Pea-hen. I think we need to have a little chat, don't we?' Mum wrapped an arm around Pea's shoulders, and swept her inside.

The desk was piled with a messy mountain of papers, as usual. Mum let out a yelp of alarm as Pea sat down, and frantically shuffled them all about so Pea couldn't possibly see any of the secret new book for grown-ups. Pea's heart sank at being shut out of the new story, but she was so worried about Sam One and Molly that there was barely room in her head.

'Now, let's get this sorted out. This is about your birthday party, isn't it?'

'How did you know?' Pea whispered.

'I'm your mum,' she said, with a twinkly smile. 'Mums know *everything*.'

So Pea explained about Bethany not liking horses any more, and how she wasn't meant to be friends with a boy, and all the other horrible things about growing up. 'And I'm trying *really* hard to be mature and sophisticated, but I don't want to have to give up everything else.'

'Oh, my poor dove,' said Mum, stroking Pea's hair. 'That's not what being grown up means. You don't have to give up anything. The most grown-up thing of all is to know what *you* like, and like it – whether what you like is horses, or not horses, or both at once. And especially if what you like is a friend.'

And that was that.

Five minutes later, it was all fixed.

Dear Ewan McGregor,

I'm not having a sleepover party any more. Mum says she's got a clever idea for a Perfectly Pea-like Party to go with my surprise present, so she is going to organize it all for me, and the party will be a surprise too.

She says Sam One will definitely be invited, so if you do come, then you don't have to worry about being the only boy.

Love from Pea xx

CHAPTER 7

THE AMAZING PEA

Friday began early – very early – with a yell of
'I AM EIGHT! AT LAST!' and hammerings on
bedroom doors.

Tinkerbell's presents were unwrapped in her
bedroom, with everyone sitting on her blue Cookie
Monster fur rug. Tinkerbell sat perched on the bed
like a tiny queen.

Pea gave her a book called *1000 Awful Jokes*.

From Clover she got a small box of modelling
clay, the sort that goes hard in the oven.

Mum's present was biggest, and saved for last.
When Tinkerbell ripped off the bright yellow paper,

she revealed a black top hat, velvety to the touch, and filled to the brim with everything a young magician might need: a black magic wand with white tips; playing cards – some real, some trick ones with parts missing or pieces that flipped over; and a book that came with trick props attached to a plastic pouch on the front – silky handkerchiefs, and foam balls that could be hidden in the palm of your hand.

'Wow,' breathed Tinkerbell, putting the top hat reverently on her head. It was too big, and balanced on the tops of her ears, tipping over her eyes if she looked down – but it was obvious from her enormous grin that she didn't mind. She ate breakfast wearing it, reading her book of tricks.

'I'm going to learn how to make a pencil float, and how to read people's minds,' she said. 'And I might make Wuffly disappear.'

'So long as you learn how to make her reappear again,' said Mum warily. 'It is Friday the thirteenth: we need to steel ourselves for disaster.'

'For why?' asked Noelle, sniffing behind her hair.

Pea explained that Friday the thirteenth was unlucky, if you were a superstitious sort of person.

'Ah,' said Noelle. 'In France, we have special lottery for Friday thirteenth. Luck for someone, uh?'

'Can I have a lottery ticket for my birthday?' asked Tinkerbell.

'No,' said Mum. 'Maybe. Er. Ask your dad.'

Clem was travelling down later that night, and would be staying until after Tinkerbell's party the next day. Usually Pea would be thrilled to see him, but she felt a quiver of envy at the words, 'Ask your dad.' Then she felt guilty for being unkind to Clem, even if it was only in her head.

There was a small war after breakfast, when Tinkerbell discovered that she wasn't allowed to wear the hat to school – even if it was her birthday.

'She'll only be eight once, Mother, don't be

mean!' said Clover, petting the bundle under her arm. (Marko's last task was for Clover to carry around a screaming baby all day. In *Alice in Wonderland* the baby was actually a pig; the closest thing in Tinkerbell's old soft toy collection was a zebra, which they'd all agreed was near enough.) When Pea and Clover left, Tinkerbell was still sitting on the floor in school uniform (plus hat), with fat tears rolling down her cheeks, while Mum insisted that tantrums were only for seven-year-olds, and completely not allowed for the eight-plus age range.

Molly was waiting for Pea at the Greyhope's gates, a big smile on her face. 'I can definitely come to your party now!' she said. 'Your mum phoned my mum last night, and then she phoned my dad, and he's going to pick me up at the end and we'll go straight to his flat like normal.'

'So – you know what my party is?'

'Oh no. Your mum told my mum it was a big secret. All I know is that it'll be at your house.'

Pea's insides felt wriggly. There were only fifteen days to wait until she would be the one unwrapping things. Now that Mum was in charge, it couldn't come soon enough.

When they got home after school, the new eight-year-old in the family was happily wearing her top hat – along with a brand-new yellow Kensal Rise Kites football shirt, with TINKERBELL and an 8 on the back in blue. It was her present from Clem.

'All right, then, my gorgeous girls – how are you doing, eh?' he said, giving Clover a peck on the cheek and a quick hug, then stooping a little to wrap his arms around Pea.

He smelled like strong tea, and custard-cream crumbs, and something else that might have been their old flat in Tenby – or perhaps it was just Clem. His curly dark hair tickled her cheek. His arms felt nice and warm, and his jumper was soft. Pea hugged him back, very tightly.

They had pasta for dinner (the soggy sort, made by Mum). Tinkerbell spent it plucking coins out of Clem's ears and getting him to guess which cup the ball was under (which he got wrong every time). Everyone found it funny – except Noelle, who sighed so hard over the football-shaped birthday cake that she almost blew out Tinkerbell's candles herself.

Clem – who was the sort of person who liked everyone, and couldn't stand the idea that anyone wasn't having a nice time – got Noelle to teach him some French while they ate cake. Most of the things he wanted to say were the same as English, like 'pizza', but it made Noelle giggle in a squeaky high-pitched way. Pea suddenly realized she'd never heard that sound before.

'Thank you,' Pea whispered to Clem later, when they were stacking things in the dishwasher. 'For cheering up Noelle, I mean. I've been trying but I'm not very good at it.'

Clem puffed out his cheeks. 'Oh, she's a nice girl

behind all that hair and sniffing, I reckon. She just misses her family, same as me. Hey, I don't know if I'll be able to make it down again for this surprise party of yours – did your mum say? It's tricky with work, with all these birthdays so close together. I'll come if I can.'

'It's OK,' said Pea quietly. 'I understand.'

That night, once she was in her pyjamas, Pea fetched her best writing pen. She *still* couldn't find her rainbow notebook, so she turned over one of her other Better Letters, and wrote on the back:

Dear Ewan McGregor,
Maybe you shouldn't come to my birthday after all because Clem might come, even though he probably can't, and although he isn't really my dad, he sort of is, a lot more than you. He knows my shoe size and why I don't like eating prawns ever, without having to be explained

to. And I know his favourite football team and
what kind of shower gel he likes, and it is just
easier because he isn't new.

Love from Pea xx

P.S. About the prawns: it is because once I
found one in my dinner with a black wiggly thing
on it like a spine, but Mum said prawn intestines
are on the outside so it was basically prawn
poo. Urgh. I have not found any more prawn
poo in my dinner, but I try not to revisit the
memory, as it upsets me. I am just telling you in
case we ever accidentally ran into each other
in a prawn-ish location.

P.P.S. I like prawn-cocktail flavour crisps,
though.

The next day was Saturday, the day of Tinkerbell's birthday party.

The morning was quiet and calm. Clover went to an all-day *Alice* rehearsal, brimful of thoughts about savage emotional underbellies. Clem took Tinkerbell and Sam Two to the local pool for a pre-party swim. Noelle went to her lesson with Tansy, mumbling, 'Hey, how are *you*? Hey, how *are* you?' under her breath. Pea finished her library book and, with nothing new to read, ended up with her nose in Tinkerbell's book of tricks.

After lunch, it was all hands on deck.

Tinkerbell and Sam Two were sent to walk Wuffly and Surprise around Queen's Park with Dr Skidelsky until the beeping alarm of Tinkerbell's watch went off.

Mum stood on a ladder and tied red and black balloons to all the lampshades.

Clem made Jamaican patties with spicy orange pastry, and buttered piles of bread for sandwiches.

Noelle put chunks of cheese and pineapple

on little sticks, with an expression of dismay.

Pea was tasked with creating a 'stage' in the front room for the magician, the Amazing Sylvester. They rigged up a blanket a metre in front of the windows, draped over a bit of a tent frame borrowed from the Paget-Skidelskys' attic. They drew the curtains, so it would be dark. Dramatic lighting was provided by the fairy lights from the Christmas box, set to maximum twinkle.

'Is it all right?' asked Pea when the puppy walkers returned.

'It's *brilliant*,' said Tinkerbell. 'The Amazing Sylvester will love it.'

Surprise yapped his agreement, turned in a circle, and did a celebratory wee up Dr Skidelsky's ankle.

'Horrible creature!' she wailed, hauling him away down the crazy paving.

By the time the party guests arrived, the hallway was happily puppy-wee-free, and all was ready. Tinkerbell had invited all her class at school, including four Olivers, three Olivias, Blonde Annabel, New Annabel, and a Horatio. She greeted them all dressed in her top hat, with a neat black outfit of trousers and a borrowed waistcoat, topped off by a red bow tie and a matching red satin band around her waist, which she proudly informed everyone was called a 'cumberbatch'. (Pea wasn't sure this was correct, but it seemed unkind to say so at her party.)

The Olivers, Olivias and Annabels – plus Sam Two – all sat expectantly on the floor of the front room. Tinkerbell sat in the middle of the first row, quivering with anticipation.

'What's that blanket for?' whispered Horatio.

'The Amazing Sylvester's going to magically appear from behind it, probably in a puff of smoke,' said Tinkerbell, with confidence.

There was a chorus of oohs.

Pea looked behind the blanket. There was nothing there.

Mum appeared in the doorway, frantically

beckoning. Pea tiptoed awkwardly across the packed room, trying not to tread on any ankles, to join her.

'Disaster!' hissed Mum. 'The Amazing Sylvester just rang me. His car's broken down! On his way back from another job in Cambridge!'

'Does that mean he's going to be a bit late?' asked a small voice.

Pea turned to find Tinkerbell standing behind her, eyes wide.

'Oh, Tink, I'm so sorry,' said Mum, dropping to her knees. 'He can't get a train or a taxi, and even if he did, it would take for ever to get here. I'm afraid there won't be any magic today.'

Tinkerbell's eyes welled with tears.

'Don't cry, babes,' said Clem, hurrying out of the kitchen and wrapping an arm around her shoulder. 'We could have a kickabout in the back garden instead, eh?'

But Tinkerbell shook her head, her mouth set in a wobbly but determined line.

Pea understood completely. Clover was right: Tinkerbell would only ever be eight once. Pea might not have known what she wanted to do on *her* birthday, but Tinkerbell had been looking forward to hers for months. To have anything other than a magical party was too cruel.

'Maybe you could do a trick or two, Tink?' said Mum, tapping the top hat. 'From your birthday set?'

But Tinkerbell shook her head again, even more firmly. 'It's *my* birthday party,' she sniffed. 'I can't be the magician at my own birthday party – I have to be the one who the magician does all the best tricks on. Those are the *rules*!'

'You were reading that book of tricks earlier,' said Clem, looking at Pea. 'You could do it.'

'What?' said Pea. 'No! I mean, I haven't practised any of the tricks, I only know how they're supposed to work. Well, a bit. That's not the same.'

Besides, Clover was the performer in the family. Pea hated being on any sort of stage.

But Tinkerbell's eyes were already shining. 'Yes please,' she whispered, taking off the beloved top hat and pressing it into Pea's hands. 'Yes please thank you very much.'

Moments later, Pea found herself behind the blanket curtain, dressed in cumberbatch and top hat, listening to the increasingly impatient whispering of the party guests. Clem, who had promised to be her 'glamorous assistant', was behind the blanket too, along with the toaster out of the kitchen.

'What's that for?' she hissed.

'You'll see,' Clem whispered back, putting two thick slices of bread in and pushing down the lever.

'Ladies and gentlemen, boys and girls!' came Mum's voice from the other side of the blanket. 'Please give a very warm and special welcome to . . . er . . . the Amazing Pea!'

The twinkly fairy lights flicked on. The blanket dropped. The toaster went *ping* – and Pea found herself appearing in a puff of smoke, just as Tinkerbell had requested.

'Yay!' yelled Tinkerbell, clapping wildly.

Everyone else clapped too. Pea mostly coughed, and then the smoke alarm went off, so they had to wait until Mum had got the ladder while Sam Two wrestled a barking Wuffly into the kitchen. When the toast smog cleared, there was Tinkerbell in the front row with her mouth open, gazing up at Pea with absolute faith.

'For her first trick,' Clem announced, 'the Amazing Pea will make handkerchiefs appear from the palm of her hand!'

Pea hadn't had any time to practise, but she did what the book had said, and – almost like magic – a huge string of bright hankies seemed to bloom from inside her own skin. She was so surprised to see it work that she did it a second time, and everyone clapped even harder.

'Thank you, thank you,' said Pea, bowing, and beginning to enjoy the feeling of being watched by smiling faces. (The top hat rolled off her head when she bent forward, but Blonde Annabel picked it up and gave it back.)

When she looked round to start the next trick, Clem was no longer standing beside her – though there was a large lumpy shape hidden behind the curtain, and a pair of big feet sticking out at the bottom.

'Next!' came Clem's voice from behind the curtain. 'The Amazing Pea will perform a card trick, the like of which you have never seen before! For this trick, she will need a volunteer from the audience!'

Tinkerbell's hand shot up, but Pea chose a small girl near the back. She had thick brown hair, startling blue eyes, and was wearing jeans and a plain, boyish sort of top just like Pea's own. 'What's your name?'

'Megan,' said the girl, nervously nibbling her bottom lip.

'Um. OK. For this trick, Megan,' said Pea, her

voice still croaky from the toast smoke, 'you must choose a card from this pack. Now, show it to the audience.'

Megan held up the card so everyone could see – except Pea, who put a hand over her eyes. But there was suddenly a lot of giggling from the audience, and when Pea sneaked a peep, she could see a lumpy shape moving along behind the curtain, as Clem made his way across the window into a better place to see the card. His head poked out as he peered over Megan's shoulder.

'Seen it!' he whispered, far too loudly.

The lumpy shape began the slow process of getting back to its original hiding place – accompanied by more giggling.

'Er . . . please place the card back into the pack,' said Pea. 'Now I will guess your secret card.'

'Four of clubs,' whispered Clem – again, far too loudly.

The book had said that, at this point, Pea was supposed to press her fingertips to her forehead and pretend to be magically reading Megan's mind – but everyone was giggling so much that it didn't seem worth it.

'Was it the four of clubs?' she asked.

'No,' said Megan, looking mortified.

'Oh, sorry,' came the muffled voice from behind the curtains. 'It's pretty dark in here, you know.'

The giggling erupted into full laughter, Tinkerbell's the loudest of all.

'A round of applause for the volunteer!' shouted Clem – and everyone clapped wildly, Pea included, as Megan smiled and sat down.

Now that she knew no one would mind if the tricks went wrong (and in fact, they quite liked it if they did), Pea's confidence swelled. True, she dropped the egg she was meant to be plucking out of New Annabel's ear, and discovered why the book suggested using boiled ones. Yes, she forgot to do the trick part of 'Find the Lady' where you tucked the little foam ball in your hand instead of under one of three cups, so that Sam Two guessed it right three times. But she really *did* make Mum's favourite ring hover up and down the magic wand, without any assistance from behind the curtain.

The Amazing Pea was a hit.

All that was left was the grand finale.

'And now, ladies and gentlemen, boys and girls,' boomed Clem, 'the Amazing Pea will make the birthday girl disappear!'

Tinkerbell bounced up to join Pea, beaming out at the audience.

'Have you read this bit of the book yet?' whispered Pea, while everyone was clapping.

'No, I didn't get that far,' said Tinkerbell. 'Does that matter?'

'Not really. But listen very carefully to Clem in a minute and do what he says, or it'll look rubbish.'

Tinkerbell stood centre stage, and Mum even found a torch to shine on her so she was in a spotlight. Then Pea draped the blanket back over the tent frame, so that Tinkerbell was hidden from the audience.

'Now, everyone, I shall have to say the magic words and concentrate very hard – but I will also need your help. First, I need you to all say *Whoosh!* On the count of three: one, two, three . . .'

The crowd *Whooshed.*

If there happened to be another whooshing noise and some loud whispering, perhaps coming from behind the curtain, at that exact same time, no one heard it.

'Is everything all right in there, birthday girl?' asked Pea. 'Knock three times if it is!'

The blanket rippled outwards three times, as if being tapped by Tinkerbell.

'Good. Now, to make you begin to vanish, we must all say another magic word: *Bing-bong!* On the count of three: one, two, three . . .'

'*Bing-bong!*' went the audience.

It was possible that there was another noise, quite like it, that seemed to come from somewhere else in the house. But if so, no one noticed – apart from Mum, who said she had to just pop out of

153

the room for a second to check the birthday candles were ready.

'Nearly time for cake, Tinkerbell,' said Pea. 'Knock twice if you're looking forward to cake?'

The blanket rippled twice, but more faintly this time.

'Now, are you ready? One last magic word: *Ta-da*. One, two, three . . .'

'*Ta-da!*' chorused the crowd.

At the moment they said it, Pea made the blanket drop – and Tinkerbell had vanished.

Everyone gasped.

'Ta-da!' said Pea again, pointing at the back of the room – and there, in the doorway, quite impossibly, stood Tinkerbell, grinning fit to burst.

The audience were still applauding when Mum arrived with the birthday cake – two chocolate Swiss rolls glued together, with white icing on each end so it looked like a magic wand, jelly tots for magic sparkle, and eight candles, all burning brightly.

Everyone was too busy singing 'Happy Birthday'

to ask how the trick was done – although when Clover was dropped home from her rehearsal, she demanded, 'Why are the curtains shut when the window at the front of the house is wide open? And the front door. Aren't you all cold?'

'Oh, is that Marko?' asked Mum, peering out into the street. 'Why don't you invite him in for cake too?'

There was a silver minibus hovering in the road, waiting to be sure Clover was safely home; Pea could just make out Marko's pointy beard, and a clutch of other students who were being dropped off afterwards. But with an unexpected glare, Clover slammed the door, and hurried upstairs without a word.

Later, when everyone had gone home with their party bags, Tinkerbell brought Pea a slice of cake.

'I saved you one of the end bits, because it's got the most icing and jelly tots,' she said shyly, 'to say thank you for being Amazing.'

Pea smiled. 'Was it all right? I hope I didn't

spoil the tricks in your book for you. You can still do them on the rest of us – I won't tell anyone how they're done. And I'm sorry I wasn't as good as a *real* magician.'

Tinkerbell shook her head and beamed. 'Everyone saw the Amazing Sylvester at Angelo's party already. Having you instead was tons better. Best birthday ever!'

'Too right,' said Clem, coming to give Pea a hug goodbye.

'I couldn't have done it at all without you,' whispered Pea, squeezing him tight.

'Don't you forget it!' he said. 'What a team: the Amazing Pea and the Lumpy Curtain Man.' He gave her a wink, and blew them all kisses as he got into his taxi.

Pea ate her slice of cake sitting on the blanket in the half-darkness, looking at the twinkly lights. They *had* made a good team; an amazing team. She didn't think a pirate or a rock climber could've been anywhere near as good.

She didn't need Ewan McGregor, not really. If he so wanted to be lost, he could stay lost. She had all the Dad she could possibly want.

With a happy sigh, Pea took down the twinkly lights, and bundled up the blanket. She packed away the magic tricks, and took the tent frame out into the hallway for the Paget-Skidelskys to collect.

On the hall table was an open box of 'Marinamail' – letters for Marina Cove from her adoring fans, parcelled up and sent on by the Dreaditor's office. Perched on top of the pile of letters in the box was an envelope addressed to:

PRUDENCE LLEWELLYN

with c/o MARINA COVE underneath, printed on a sticky label.

Curious, Pea padded upstairs to her bedroom, then peeled open the flap and pulled out a type-written letter on thick creamy paper.

Dear Prudence,

I hope this letter finds you well.
Please allow me to introduce
myself: I am a businessman, and
I travel occasionally through
the city of London. On my most
recent visit, I read a magazine containing an article about
a writer of children's books.
The photograph caught my eye,
as it looked a lot like an old
friend of mine. When I read the
article, I realized it was the
same Bree Llewellyn I knew years
before, in Greece.

The last time I saw her she
was holding a baby. I think that
baby was you. If so, I am your
father.

I apologize if this letter
is a shock to you. I have tried

to find you in the past, to
explain my behavior, but with no
success. When I saw the article
I decided to write via the
publisher of the books. I did
not want to contact your mother;
I'm sure you are clever enough
to understand.

I am so sorry for not being a
better father. I hope you have a
very happy birthday.

Affectionately,

EM

Ewan McGregor

CHAPTER 8

DEAR PRUDENCE

Pea sat on the end of her bed, clutching the letter.

She re-read it three times, her heart skipping uncertainly in her chest, faster each time.

She stared at *Prudence*, and *I think that baby was you*, and *I am so sorry*. Her fingertip traced the inky swirl of the signature: *E M*, in dark blue. She lifted it up to her face, closed her eyes, and pressed the soft creamy paper to her cheek, just for a second; believed it, just for one more second.

Then she shook herself, folded the letter back into its envelope, and quietly summoned Clover and Tinkerbell up to her room.

'Which one of you was it?' Pea asked in a low whisper, making sure the door was closed tight.

Clover had flung herself back onto Pea's pillows, and was irritably coiling a twirl of hair around her forefinger. Tinkerbell was fiddling with the ribbon on her top hat.

'Which one of us did what?' demanded Clover.

Pea held up the envelope. 'I know it can't be real,' she said, wishing her voice didn't sound so small and sad. 'I know it's not really from him, and you're just trying to be kind, but it's made me feel all funny on the inside – so please don't.'

'What are you floffling on about?' said Tinkerbell, screwing up her face as she read the envelope. 'We wouldn't send you a letter to *Prudence*. No one calls you that.'

'We wouldn't send you a letter at all,' said Clover, swinging her legs off the bed and plucking the envelope from Pea's hand.

Pea watched, trembling, as she read the letter,

with Tinkerbell peering over her shoulder, waiting for a telltale glance between them or a guilty blush on their cheeks. But none came; only a gasp from Clover, who covered her mouth with her hand and stared at Pea with huge blue eyes.

'Oh, *Pea*,' she breathed.

Clover was a very good actor, but mainly the sort where you watched them and thought, *What good acting that actor is doing there*, rather than really believing they were someone else. It didn't look as if she were pretending.

'Tink?' said Pea, feeling dizzy. 'Was it you, all by yourself? Or maybe with Sam Two helping with the writing?'

Tinkerbell was a practised liar, but when she lied, she had explanations on the tip of her tongue: for why the blob of Nutella on the new red sofa was definitely not connected to the smear of Nutella on her cheek, or how Wuffly's blue tail was a common sign of dog-fever, and nothing to do with the WET PAINT sign on the newsagent's blue door. A silent.Tinkerbell was generally an honest one. And Tinkerbell said not one word.

Pea sat down on the fuzzy old carpet with a thump. She realized her mouth was hanging open in a big round O, but somehow it wouldn't close – as if the idea of the letter was too big for her body to hold inside it.

'Why would you think it was from us?' asked Tinkerbell, frowning.

Pea blushed. 'Because it's too perfect. It's what I wanted, exactly: a letter from my dad that said sorry. No one ever gets exactly what they want. Not in real life, anyway.'

It happened in books all the time. If Mum's mermaids imagined in Chapter One how nice it would be to skip mer-school and sneak off in a boat to Starfish Island, you could guarantee that by Chapter Three they would be hoisting the sails. But Mum hadn't written *their* lives. It was far too good to be true.

But Clover was smiling. 'No, don't you see?

That's what makes it so fantastic! Anyway, how could it possibly be a fake? We didn't make it, and no one but us knows you've been looking for him, do they?'

'Sam One does,' said Pea reluctantly – for it was very much the sort of kind, thoughtful thing he might do – though she shook her head immediately. 'But I don't think he'd be able to write that by himself. His spelling isn't very businessman-like.'

'That settles it,' said Clover. 'No one else knows all this stuff – about Greece, and him leaving when you were just born. Your dad's name: no one would guess that. He knows it's nearly your birthday. And Mum *did* do that interview, remember? He could easily have seen it. Look, he's even spelled *behavior* wrong, like Americans do. Pea, this is real. It must be. A real letter from your real long-lost father.' Clover's eyes filled with tears, and her hand crept over to stroke the face of the oversized watch on her other wrist.

Pea clutched her thumbs very tightly.

'Why does it say he's a businessman?' asked

Tinkerbell, suddenly all suspicion. 'He's got that bit wrong; he definitely used to be a pirate.'

Clover and Pea exchanged grins.

'You know we made that up, Tink,' said Pea, 'as an excuse for why he ran away. It's like being a lion tamer, or an astronaut. Probably someone somewhere has to be one, but it's not a very likely sort of job for an actual grown-up dad person.'

'He's probably rich,' said Clover, perking up at once. 'He'll have a pinstriped suit, and a massive car with leather seats, and a secretary. Houses all over the world. A yacht!'

'Woo-hoo!' said Tinkerbell. 'What's a yacht?'

'A swanky boat for snotty rich people.'

'My dad won't be a snotty rich person!' said Pea, not sounding quite as certain as she would like.

'He might be,' Clover warned. 'He might smoke cigars and wear a cowboy hat. And under the hat he's bald.'

Tinkerbell nodded gleefully. 'An old fat man in a suit, who wears a wig on his fat bald head!'

'Stop it!' said Pea, slapping her hand on the carpet. 'Don't! It was funny to make him up, before – but now he's a real person, and he's got swirly handwriting, and a pen with blue ink, and . . . Well, I don't really know many details apart from those, but still. Imagine if we all made fun of Clem.'

'Sorry,' mumbled Tinkerbell.

'Very sorry,' said Clover.

'Anyway, we'll find out what he looks like when he comes to your birthday party,' Tinkerbell added.

Pea shivered, a thrill running down her spine. It was really going to happen. He really *was* going to be on the doorstep, on her birthday.

Then she clapped her hands to her mouth. 'No! We can't *actually* invite him. I mean, I know we talked about it, but – he's a stranger. Well, nearly. You never tell strangers where you live; there's a display on the notice board in the library. You're supposed to report them to a responsible adult. Do I have to report him to a responsible adult if he's my dad as well as a stranger? They didn't put that on the poster.'

'Whoa, slow down!' said Clover. 'You're right, you can't invite him to our house. Not yet. I mean, he definitely completely absolutely *is* your real dad, but we still have to make sure. If you're worried about baldness, you can ask him to send you his picture when you write back. You *are* going to write back, aren't you?'

'Yes,' said Pea, her heart in her mouth, thinking of the letters she'd already written and hidden away in her bedside drawer. 'But. Um. I need to think for a bit. It has been my whole entire life since we last saw each other. I want to make sure the first words I ever write to him are the best ones ever.'

'We could help?' offered Tinkerbell.

But Pea shook her head. This she would have to do by herself.

One full hour of sucking her pen and doodling in the margins instead of writing words later, Pea had written a letter.

Dear E M,*

Your letter made me very happy, and not shocked. I think I was that baby too. Do you like The Beatles?

I have lots of questions for you, but if you are a businessman you probably don't have time to read a big long letter, so here are my most important ones:

- Could you email me a photograph of yourself? (I promise not to mind if you are bald.)
- Which Greek island did you meet my mum on?
- Where have you been?

Please write back very very soon, as soon as possible. When will you be in London again?

Love from Pea** xx***

* I have put E M because Dad sounds a bit forward and peculiar, and Mr McGregor

sounds horrible and rabbit-killerish. I hope you understand.

** Everyone calls me Pea now, not Prudence.

*** I sign all my letters with two kisses, in case that looks forward and peculiar as well.

She read it over carefully, checking for spelling mistakes. Then she took it to show the others. 'Perfect,' said Clover.

'I get all the little stars mixed up with the kisses,' said Tinkerbell, 'but I like the bullet points.'

Pea beamed. It felt like the perfect introduction: friendly, but not too friendly. She'd thought about adding in something about prawns, but it seemed best to stick to the most important things. There would be time for prawns later.

But when she checked Ewan McGregor's letter,

she realized there was no return address to send her reply to. There was nothing on the envelope either; not even a postmark to show where it had travelled from. With a sigh, she tucked her letter away in her drawer with all the other unpostable Better Letters – but only temporarily. She'd find a way to send this one, she knew it. E M had been in London. E M had written to her, and wished her happy birthday, and been *so sorry*. He wanted her to find him.

All she had to do was work out *how*.

Sunday morning was usually a lazy, sleepy affair – but not today.

Tinkerbell was wearing stripy pyjamas with her top hat, and periodically yelled '*Fetcho raspberry jammius!*' and '*Unburnify toasticorn!*' at the breakfast things.

Wuffly leaped off her blue blanket at every wave of the magic wand, and bounded around the table barking.

And after Clem's visit, Noelle was so perky she

was actually whistling. True, it was still from behind her hair curtains, and it wasn't very loud – but it was undeniably cheerful. She was even wearing a top that was a light enough shade of brown to be almost golden.

Clover, however, flopped down the stairs late with her shoulders drooping, ignored the cereal boxes, and poured herself a cup of black coffee. Then she added three spoonfuls of sugar – and would've added more if Mum hadn't taken the spoon away with a frown.

'Is this another Alice thing?' asked Tinkerbell.

'I don't remember Alice turning into a sugar-mad floppy fourteen-year-old in the book,' said Mum.

'Pfft. Stupid Alice,' muttered Clover.

Mum looked pained. 'Oh, my flower. Did yesterday's rehearsal not go very well? With all the birthday stuff going on, I didn't ask.'

Guiltily, Pea realized that she hadn't asked either.

Clover confirmed that rehearsals had indeed not been quite as she'd hoped. Marko's clever

171

new vision for the play involved a puppet Alice, to 'enhance the surreal dream-like quality of the audience experience'. This meant that Clover, far from having the main role, was to be asleep for the entire production, apart from the very beginning and end. Almost every line she'd learned had been cut. And – apparently most upsettingly – her traditional Alice costume of blue dress and hair ribbon was to be replaced: first by scruffy jeans and a T-shirt, and then, during the 'dreaming' parts, by a sort of slithery grey body-stocking.

'I'll look like a slug. A lumpy grey slug with no lines.'

'And after you spent all that time sitting in a wardrobe,' said Tinkerbell, sympathetically waving her magic wand. 'Shall I turn *him* into a slug?'

'Please do,' sighed Clover.

'Well, I think it sounds very . . . creative,' said Mum. 'I expect Marko just wants you to try something new, that's all. Every artist needs to stay fresh. Now, give me that coffee, have some proper breakfast, and then shoo – I've got work to do. Why don't you see what the Sams are up to?'

Pea got dressed at once. She couldn't wait to show Sam One the letter. He was bound to have good ideas for tracking down missing E Ms with loopy signatures.

But when she knocked, he wasn't even allowed to come to the door. Pea had to go out to the back garden, climb up onto a patio table, and peer over the brick wall.

'Sorry,' said Sam One, squinting up at her awkwardly. 'Surprise ate twenty-six pages of Mum K's research notes, and did a wee in the washing machine. No screen time except for homework, and we can't have friends round.'

It felt very odd, explaining to the top of Sam One's head about getting a real letter from her real dad. She gripped the top of the mossy brick wall tightly, just in case a telltale guilty look was about to flash across his eyes – but he looked as honestly shocked as Clover and Tinkerbell had.

'Are you sure it's not an imposter?' he said, his narrow freckly face pinching up with worry.

'That's what I'm trying to check!' said Pea. 'My letter back's got a clever question in it that only the real him would know the answer to. But if I can't send it—'

There was a howl from inside the house next door – a doggy one – followed by another that was distinctly human. A moment later, Surprise came bounding out of the back door, a slice of pepperoni pizza in his jaws. He ran in a mad circle, dropped the pizza on Sam One's shoe, then made a leap for the climbing frame. By the time Dr Skidelsky came charging out after him, he was dangling off the swing by his little jaws.

'I'd better go,' said Sam One, staring unhappily at the pepperoni on his trainer. 'Good luck!'

'You too,' said Pea, ducking out of sight and wobbling off the table as Dr Skidelsky shouted the sort of words that even grown-ups usually looked startled at.

Dear Prudence

Pea went upstairs to re-read EM's letter for the hundredth time. Then, too excited to resist, she took out her notepaper again.

Dear Ewan McGregor,
Getting a letter from you made me the happiest person in the whole world.

I've actually been writing Better Letters to you for ages, but from now on I'm going to write you real letters. I don't know where to post them to, but I will soon. I might even be able to give them to you in person. Anyway I thought it would be helpful for you to read all about me beforehand, and that way any time we have together will be saved for important/ fun things.

Actually, you can sort of read all about me in Mum's books, because she based the character Coraly on me. I have curly red hair

like her. But I'm not a mermaid and I haven't
died or come back as a ghost, so don't
expect me to be those things.

I'm not sure what to write now.

Thank you for wishing me a happy birthday.
It's still quite far away so there is time for you
to buy me a present, if you wanted. I would
quite like a watch, but if that's too expensive,
then you could choose me a book or some
pens, maybe?

Love from
Pea
(Pea is what everyone calls me, not Prudence,
I can explain why later)

After a moment's thought, she crossed out *Love
from*, and put:

~~Love from~~ Best wishes,
Pea xx

Biting her lip, she scribbled out the 'xx' too. Then she added back just one 'x', so it was friendly, but not quite as friendly as she usually was – to make it absolutely clear that she was both pleased to hear from him, but still a little bit cross about all the years with no birthday presents.

~~Love from~~ Best wishes,
Pea ●● x

With a satisfied smile, she folded the letter. The rainbow notebook was still missing, so she took out a fresh sheet of paper. She would start a new Amy story; one especially for him.

In the land of Moriana lived a princess. Her name was Amethyst, but everyone called her Amy. She liked riding horses, fishing and other outdoor pursuits such as rock climbing. Her trusty friend Batthew was always at her side or flapping around her head. (Batthew was a bat.)

One day, Amy heard a tapping at the castle window (even though it didn't have any glass because that hadn't been invented yet). There was a huge black raven on the windowsill, with a tiny scroll of paper attached to its leg.

'Oh no!' cried Amy as she unfurled the scroll. 'King Redbeard has been kidnapped! Wake up, Batthew, we must rescue him!'

'Do we have to? I'm sleepy,' said Batthew, putting his wings over his furry face. (Bats are nocturnal so they had this sort of conversation a lot.)

'Of course! We must solve the riddle this raven has brought us to find him.'

Follow the path carved by dragon's breath
Into the eye
Where the flamingos walk

Pea sucked the end of her pen. It was a good story so far, and she liked the *dragon's breath* clue, but the flamingos seemed out of place. She changed it to:

Where the ~~flamingos walk~~ roses bloom

– but that sounded a bit romantic. After more thinking, and crossing out, and thinking again, it looked like:

Where the ~~flamingos walk~~ ~~roses bloom~~
wolves howl ~~in the moonlight~~ The ~~moonlight~~
will show ~~light~~ the ~~path~~ way

It looked awful. Even Pea could hardly read some of the words. Usually she wouldn't care – it was her story, after all – but this one was for E M. It was meant to be perfect.

She looked at her letter, and the scribbled-out kisses. That didn't look good either, so she turned the scribbles into daisies.

~~Love from~~ Best wishes,
Pea❀❀x

Now she was reading it over, the rest of the letter wasn't perfect either. Was it rude to ask for a present? It might be. The last thing she wanted was for him to think she was rude – but she couldn't scribble all of that out and cover it with a daisy.

Dear Ewan McGregor,

I don't know when I will give you this letter, but I wanted to write you some things so you will know about me, in case you want to know about me.

Things I like: books, writing, knowing exactly what time it is.

Things I don't like: prawns, 1-Click Dream, people calling me 'Ginger', 'Carrots', etc.

I am more things than this, but that will do to start with.

Love from Pea xx

This time she thought hard before putting *Love from* and two kisses, so she wouldn't have to do more scribbling out. But when she compared the two letters, she squeaked and picked up her pen again at once.

Dear Ewan McGregor,
I forgot to say in my other letter that I was
very very happy to get a letter from you. I
said it the first time and then I forgot, but
I thought it was important for you to know
so that you know you should maybe send me
another one (perhaps with your address on).
Please.

Love from Pea xx

She quite wanted to write another letter
apologizing for writing too many letters, but she
decided that finding out where to send them was
probably more urgent.

She fetched E M's letter, and tried very hard to
think Young Sherlock Holmes-ish thoughts about it
instead of fondly staring at the blue inky signature.
If only it had been written on a typewriter, the sort

with a wonky 'e' that would give him away; if only the ink were an unusual shade of blue that only one shop in all of London would sell. But it wasn't. Pea's heart skipped a beat when she found a name embossed on the flap of the envelope – but it said W H SMITH, and there were millions of those. There were no clues. It was just a letter, printed on plain creamy paper like the sort Mum used.

Pea went on staring at it all afternoon.

'Ugh,' said Tinkerbell, disgusted, when Pea turned down the offer of being in a cardboard box while the Amazing Tinkerbell poked knives into it. 'You're even more boring than Clover.'

'I'm a slug,' moped Clover. 'I'm supposed to be dull.'

'Can we help you look for Peter Rabbit clues instead?' asked Tinkerbell.

'Yes please,' said Pea. 'I'm completely stuck. I thought maybe there might be a code hidden in the first letter of each sentence, but DIPOTW doesn't mean anything.'

'It's a shame there's not more handwriting,' said Clover, eyeing the letter. 'You can tell a lot about someone from the way they do their *f*s, apparently. Not that there are any *f*s in "Ewan McGregor". Funny how he didn't write his whole name, though.'

'Maybe that's a clue?' said Pea hopefully.

'Yeah!' said Tinkerbell. 'He might be ill. Like, with a cold and a headache so he got someone else to do typing. Or maybe his travelling-on-business plane crashed and his hands are all mashed up, and he's hit his head so he's forgotten his own name—'

'Tink!' said Clover.

Tinkerbell looked guilty. 'Colds happen more often than plane crashes,' she said, patting Pea's hand. 'I'm sure his hands aren't really mashed up.'

Pea looked at her fingers: pale, short and stubby. Mum's fingers were long and elegant; nothing like hers. She pictured her father holding

184

a shiny fountain pen to sign E M – and though his were larger, obviously, with some manly hairy bits and businesslike cuffs round his wrists, she was certain they'd be just like hers. He probably had freckles on the backs of his hands too.

'But why didn't he put his address?' she said.

Tinkerbell patted her hand again. 'He probably just forgot. You know what grown-ups are like. Mum forgot to change out of her pyjama bottoms when she went to the shop earlier. Clem left one of his socks under the sofa. They're all useless.'

'Actually,' said Clover reluctantly, 'I can think of another reason he might not have wanted you to write back . . .'

'It's me, isn't it?' said Pea in a small voice. 'There's something wrong with *me*.'

'No!' Clover leaned forward and lowered her voice. 'Only . . . well, this is a guess, but – maybe you aren't his only daughter? He knew Mum years ago. He could've got married. He might have a

185

whole other family by now. And maybe he needs to talk to them first. Or he could be trying to keep you a secret?'

Pea felt a knot in her throat, so tight she could barely breathe.

Another family.

Other children, as well as her. Other children who he was a proper dad to. He wouldn't want her at all.

It was too much. She clutched her thumbs, but a sob burst out of her mouth.

'I don't see why you're upset,' grumbled Tinkerbell. 'You might have, like, ten new brothers and sisters. Think how many birthday presents you'll get now!'

But Clover – who was quite red-eyed herself – was very stern. 'It's not like that at all, Tink. Imagine if it was you, and Clem suddenly told *you* that you weren't his only baby. Imagine if you had an extra sister all of a sudden: someone who was in your family, and you didn't even know them at all, and suddenly you were supposed to think about them just like me and Pea.'

Tinkerbell chewed the inside of her cheek. 'That happened to Blonde Annabel. Her mum married a new man, and then her dad married a new woman, and she's got three brothers from her stepdad, and a brother and a sister from the stepmum. The brother and the sister are called Milan and Paris and they're only four. And she has to share a bedroom with them.'

'See?' said Clover. 'And it must be just as weird for Milan and Paris and all the rest.'

Pea pictured her businessman in his pinstripes, quietly pushing her forward and saying, 'This, children, is my *other* daughter,' to a roomful of ten glaring figures, all with bright red hair, big chins and stubby fingers. They'd pull her hair, and call her 'Pee'. They'd make her eat prawns. And he, her father, would fly off around the world on his business trips, and never even notice.

'I think I'd like to be alone for a bit,' sniffed Pea.

Dear E M,

I'm sure you are very busy with your new life7 and maybe you don't really want an extra daughter.

~~It would still be nice if~~

~~I'd still like it if~~

Please could you send me one photograph of you, just so that I have a picture to put in the family album. We could call that my birthday present, if you like. Otherwise it's a bit like I imagined you.

With kind regards,

Pea

She slipped the new letter into her bedside drawer with the rest. Then, with a heavy sigh, she began to fold up the letter from E M, to put it back in its envelope for ever—

Pea froze.

She clicked on her desk lamp.

No, she hadn't imagined it. On the back of the letter was what looked like writing: very faint, but in the same blue ink as the loopy signature of E M.

'A clue,' she whispered to herself. 'An actual proper clue.'

9

DETECTIVE INSPECTOR PEA RETURNS

Pea fetched fresh plain paper, and carefully copied out the faint, smudgy marks from the back of EM's letter.

> REFAEDEKE HOIEL 2VI TT

It was impossible to read – Pea wasn't even sure they were letters – but that was no problem: not to a trainee Ruby Redfort or Sherlock Holmes. He'd left a set of clues for her to unravel, if only she was clever enough.

But why? Was Ewan McGregor a spy, who needed to keep his location a secret? That would explain why he'd vanished without trace all those years ago, and why Mum had never been able to find him. And now here he was, desperate to contact his long-lost Prudence, knowing it was too dangerous to simply turn up on the doorstep. He hadn't *forgotten* to write an address. He'd left it out on purpose, for her own safety, all the while hoping she might be able to *find* him.

If she was completely honest, Pea thought him being a spy was about as likely as him being a pirate. But even if that wasn't why he'd left it, she could still crack the code.

She stared at the markings, trying to make them fit together. She spun the paper round, but they didn't mean anything more upside-down. It was like a puzzle with half of it missing; letters that weren't complete.

With a gasp, Pea leaped down the attic steps to Clover's room.

'I need to borrow your little mirror,' she said, stepping gingerly over Clover – who was lying miserably on the floor, practising being a slug. 'I'll bring it back!'

Back at her desk, Pea held the mirror so that it stood up on its edge, and lined it up with the code. In one direction it just made more code – but when she moved the mirror, letters appeared:

BEᗡEDEKE HOIEᑕ ƷᛉI II

B, Es, D, a K, H, O, some Is, an S . . . There were some funny symbols as well – a diamond, some slanty lines a bit like an X – but she was definitely on the right track.

Pea wrote down the letters she could read with a trembly hand, then made guesses for the rest.

BE??EDEKE HOIE? ƷX(?)I II

She took away the mirror, and tried guessing

what the missing letters might be – if perhaps the person writing them had got capitals and lower case mixed up.

BERNEDEKE HOIER 3XI II

Was Bernedeke Hoier a friend of Ewan McGregor's? Pea had never met anyone called Bernedeke, but it sounded like it might be a real name. Looking up Ewan McGregor on the internet had been hopeless – but surely there couldn't be more than one Bernedeke Hoier?

Pea hurried downstairs, but the study was still locked; when she tried the handle, Mum poked her head out from the front room and wagged a finger with a giggle, though Pea couldn't see anything funny about it.

She couldn't ask the Paget-Skidelskys.

And Noelle's laptop was no good: she'd spent most of Sunday with it perched on her knee, chattering away in French to her family through the webcam. The one time Pea found it unguarded, resting on the kitchen table, she had furtively sat down – only to find that the webcam was still on, and there were four aunts, a grandfather and a cat with a black smudge on its nose peering back at her through the screen.

'*Je suis* . . . sorry!' squeaked Pea, in a vaguely French accent, and snapped the lid closed.

It was no good. Bernedeke Hoier would have to wait until school.

Dear Dad,
I've found your secret message and I'm working on it as fast as I can.

    I should probably write this letter in code, but you might be too busy with spy things to solve it, so this seems easier.

Love from Pea xx

It was only after she'd finished that she realized she'd written *Dear Dad*. Her pen hovered, ready to make another scribble-daisy. But, she thought, perhaps it looked quite all right after all.

'Morning!' said Miss Pond as Pea sprinted past some chatty Year Nines to get to the computers first. 'Any books I can recommend? Back to deaths instead of detectives, maybe?'

Pea mumbled something about an urgent project until Miss Pond went away.

There were Bernadettes and Benedeks on the internet, but no Bernedekes. No Hoiers, either.

It was horribly disappointing.

To improve her chances, Pea took out all

the other Ruby Redforts and Young Sherlock Holmeses from the school library, much to Miss Peel's delight.

On Tuesday, Pea tried anagrams, instead.

'What does *Eek! Reindeer Hob* mean to you?' she asked Molly, in English. 'Or *Heroine Reek Bed*?'

'It means detention for both of you, if you don't stop chattering,' snapped Mr Ellis, giving Pea a glare.

She meekly put her head down and tried to concentrate on her Non-Chronological Report, but it was awfully hard.

Pea spent all of Wednesday doodling pictures of birthday cakes on her books, and trying to turn diamonds and roman numerals into useful letters. This time Mr Ellis really did give her a detention, and Mrs Anders made her stand up in front of the whole class and do French verbs on the whiteboard for forgetting her homework.

'Don't you have a French girl living in your house?' hissed Bethany, after Mrs Anders had plucked the chunky blue marker out of Pea's hand and sent her back to her seat in disgrace.

'Ye-es,' Pea whispered back guiltily. 'But we're helping her learn English, she's not teaching me French.'

When she got home, she took the page of code out to the back garden, Wuffly at her heels, and half-heartedly kicked a ball for her to chase while staring at the clue until it went blurry under her eyes.

A series of shouts and nervous barks floated over the garden wall.

'No, I said *Roll over*! That's not rolling over, that's eating my shoelaces – why would I ever tell you to do that? Get *off*!'

As the barking got louder, Wuffly joined in. It set Surprise off into frenzied howls, accompanied by wails of dismay from Sam Two.

'Whoever's there, can you take Wuffly indoors?' called Sam One indistinctly over the wall. 'Only Surprise has gone a bit . . . werewolfy.'

Once Pea had shooed Wuffly inside, still barking, she dragged the patio table back over to the wall, and clambered up.

The next-door garden had been transformed into an obstacle course. The familiar climbing frame and monkey bars had been joined by a meandering pathway marked in white paint on the grass, like the lines on a football pitch. Surprise was bounding cheerfully around it, ignoring every white line, pursued by a red-faced Sam Two.

'Hi,' said Sam One, peering up. 'Sorry about the noise. We're supposed to show Mum K all our puppy-training progress when she gets back from Edinburgh on Saturday – or Mum Gen says she might send him away to live with another family.'

Surprise began to dig a hole in the middle of the lawn, and only stopped when Sam Two frantically dangled the squeaky carrot toy under his nose – which he snatched out of her hands, and immediately buried in the hole. Pea was not convinced Dr Skidelsky would consider that 'progress'.

'Have you found out anything more about your dad?'

Pea clung tightly to the mossy bricks as she explained – about the code, and Bernedeke Hoier, and how *Eek! Reindeer Hob* didn't mean anything. She handed her page of anagrams and questionable letters down to him, so he could see. He frowned at it as he read.

'What if it's in a foreign language?' he said.

Pea bit her lip, watching as Surprise tried to run up the slide on the climbing frame. 'He's American. I know they spell things a bit funny, but the words are mostly the same. I suppose there could be other anagrams, in French or something . . .'

'No, I meant the letters, not the words,' said Sam One. 'What if it's a different alphabet?'

'Oh. Like Chinese?' said Pea.

'Or Russian,' said Sam One. 'Or Greek?'

The patio table lurched under Pea's ankles, and she almost fell.

'Greek! Like on a Greek island!'

If Ewan McGregor had wanted to send a secret message that only she could translate, that would be the perfect way.

'Down! *Down!* Sit? No, don't poo *there*!' wailed Sam Two. 'Sam, help me!'

Sam One gave Pea an apologetic wave, and hurried across the grass.

'Thanks!' Pea called after him, wobbling off the table. 'I'll let you know what it says the second I've worked it out!'

Tinkerbell's Greece books had all gone back to the library, so Pea had an agonizing wait until Thursday morning.

'My best customer, back again,' said Miss Pond, looking Pea up and down with a frown as she juggled her keys and her coffee cup. 'Still on that *urgent project*, are we?'

'Yes. Very urgent. Need to get in. Urgently.'

She rifled through the shelves in the reference section with no luck, then hurried to the only free computer.

Sam One was right: Greek did have a different alphabet.

Pea copied down the whole thing, then spent all morning sneakily poring over Γ and Λ, Σ and Π under the desk in History, hiding in the paint room in Art.

It had to be the right track. If you only looked at the top half of the code, all the letters fitted perfectly, except for D.

'Is that some birthday thing?' asked Bethany, crinkling her nose up as she ate her daily lunch-time Wotsits (now kept in her 1-Click Dream lunchbox).

'Um,' said Pea, covering the page with her hand. 'Yes. Secret party business.'

'I thought your party was going to be a surprise?' said Molly – but Pea hurried to the library without another word.

It felt horrible lying to them. If her father really was a spy, he'd have to do that a lot, but that thought wasn't much comfort; not if it meant he might lie to *her* too.

Safe in a quiet corner, she spread out her notes and, with a shaky hand, translated the Greek letters back into the old familiar ones.

BEGLEd(?)EKE HOIEG

There were no Begledeke Hoiegs listed online.

She tried anagrams – but *Edge Hike Eel Gob* didn't sound like a clue. Neither did *Beg Godlike Eeeeh!*

She tried looking things up using the original Greek letters, ΒΕΣΛΕΔΕΚΕ ΗΟΙΕΣ – but there were no results for that. She tried putting in just a few letters, but it was confusing staring at pages that said *Τούρτα ζελέ με ροδάκινα* and *Πίτσες*, especially when, after she clicked on the translate button, they turned out to be recipes for peach cake and pizza.

If Ewan McGregor was sending her a secret message, it wasn't in Greek – or if it was, she couldn't read it.

'Still no luck?' asked Clover, seeing her drooping shoulders on the bus home.

Pea nodded miserably. 'And my birthday's only nine days away. I'm running out of time.'

Clover gave her arm a squeeze. 'Maybe it's for the best, Pea. I know we were supposed to be giving him to Mum as a surprise present – but, well, he's her rubbish ex-boyfriend who ran off and left her with two little children to look after on her own. If you think about it, that's not very present-y.'

'What? But he's my dad,' Pea protested. 'My long-lost, missing-for-years dad. It's a present for me too. She'd understand.'

And you've already got a watch from yours, so it's all right for you, she wanted to add.

'Well, I've already bought Mum something else,' said Clover. 'I think you should too.'

Pea felt utterly desolate.

She hadn't been clever enough to understand the clue in the letter. She had no idea who Ewan

McGregor was, or where he might be. Worst of all, Clover had a point: Molly's mum probably wouldn't want Molly's dad at her birthday, and they'd been properly married and everything. Mum wouldn't want Pea's dad there at all.

She slipped upstairs and, with a heavy heart, took out her notepaper for the last time.

Dear Dad,

I wish you'd never written me that letter.

Why did you bother writing it if you didn't want to meet me? All I wanted was to have a birthday present like Clover – but I think if you have a nice watch you should give it to one of the other ten children you've probably got now.

Goodbye for ever.

From Pea

At school on Friday, Pea took all her detective books back to the library. She looked so miserable that even Mr Ellis took pity on her, and let her sit out of oral presentations. (She'd drawn the topic 'The Himalayas' out of the bag; even on a good day, it would've been a challenge.)

And when she got home, it was no cheerfuller. Noelle was so drooping and tearful that the three sisters gathered nervously outside the kitchen to peer at her. She cried on some ironing. She cried in a cup of sugary tea. She cried at the offer of 'a nice bit of cheese on toast' from Tinkerbell – and not even because that meant Tinkerbell having access to sharp things and fire.

'Mum said she was on a six-week trial, looking after us,' whispered Clover. 'Do you think she's being sent back to France?'

Tinkerbell beamed. 'Does that mean Klaudia can come back and look after us instead?'

'Don't be so mean,' hissed Pea, shooing them away, and slipping onto a kitchen chair.

'Did you get bad marks on your homework for Tansy?' she asked gently, sliding a box of tissues under Noelle's hair. 'I got six out of fifty in a test once, so I know how you feel.'

Noelle took a tissue from the box, and blew her nose noisily. She said a few things too, but they were in French, and snuffly, so Pea didn't even try to translate; she just sat patiently, like she would when Clover was having a weep.

'You is good girl, Pea. Kind girl,' snuffled Noelle eventually, putting one stiff arm around Pea's shoulders in an odd half-hug. It only lasted for a moment, but Pea was touched, and felt quite tearful herself as she went up the stairs to her attic.

Her last letter to her dad was still on the desk.

Goodbye for ever, it said. Overwhelmed, she sat down, and a tear plopped off her nose onto her words. Pea pressed her hand against the letter automatically, not that it mattered if it got smudged; no one would ever read it. Sighing, she looked at the damp ink that had been transferred onto her palm, rubbing at it to clean it off.

Goodbye forever.
from Pea

She stared at it. She twisted her wrist so she could see it the other way up. Breathless, she hunted in her school bag for all her code-cracking notes.

What if it wasn't some kind of code, or Greek? What if what was on the back of the letter was never written on the letter at all – but an imprint, reversed, from another page underneath? With some letters – B, and E – it wouldn't matter. But with the others . . .

With a shaky hand, Pea wrote out the code, turning the missing parts into letters.

BELVEDEKE HOLEL SVL TT

Then she wrote it out again, flipping the letters around in her mind.

BELVEDEKE HOTEL SAT 11

She sat completely still for a moment, just looking at the words.

'SAT' had to mean Saturday.

'11' had to be the time of day.

It was a secret arrangement, for a meeting – it had to be. That was his coded message to her: a meeting tomorrow, at 11 o'clock, at a hotel – where?

Pea dashed downstairs to tap on Mum's study door. She'd make something up about homework, or—

'Oh, Pea!' Noelle's tear-stained voice drifted out from the kitchen, interspersed with sniffs. 'Your *mama*, she is at a meeting with someone . . . her name is Miss Dreaditor, I think she say? She will be late to be coming home this evening.'

There was no way into the study.

Pea hovered in the kitchen doorway.

'Would it cheer you up to, er, look at your family photographs, maybe? On your laptop?'

Noelle stilled – then suddenly began to sob even harder.

'Oh, no, I'm sorry! You have the homesick, I understand,' said Pea, pulling out more tissues. 'I didn't mean to make it worse!'

'You is kind, very kind girl,' Noelle sobbed.

Pea didn't think she was kind: not when she'd only suggested looking at Noelle's pictures so she could look up the Belvedere Hotel on the internet. She made her another cup of tea to compensate, then guiltily retreated – and was nearly mown down in the hallway by Tinkerbell, dressed in her full magician outfit: eyeliner moustache, cumberbatch and top hat, set at a jaunty angle. 'Fear not, Pea! The Amazing Tinkerbell can cheer you up! *Smileyface lipcurviness!*'

Pea shook her head. 'The only way you can

cheer me up is to get me through that locked door to Mum's computer.'

Tinkerbell beamed, skidded back down the hallway for a moment, then waggled her eyebrows, twirled her wand between her fingers, and tapped herself smartly three times on the top of her hat.

'*Appearo key-ringium!*' she said, and whipped the hat off her head in a bow.

To Pea's utter astonishment, inside the hat was a set of keys on a familiar knotty key-ring: front door, back door, and the shiny golden one for the study.

'Ta-da!' said Tinkerbell, beaming.

'Whoa, is that—? How did you—?'

Tinkerbell waved her magic wand.

'No, *really* how did you?' asked Pea, who had read the book of magic tricks and knew there wasn't one for making things appear just because you wanted them to.

Tinkerbell looked shifty. 'OK, I just found them on the hall table and stuck them under my hat when you weren't looking. Mum must have forgotten them. I told you adults were useless.'

With a shaky hand, Pea slipped the golden key into the lock, and turned it. Or tried to, at least. It wouldn't turn. With a grunt, Pea tried forcing it, tugging on the handle – and the door opened at once.

'She must have forgotten to lock it,' said Tinkerbell. 'The Dreaditor does do that to people.'

'No,' whispered Pea, 'I don't think she forgot.' The cheerful mess of notes, printouts and Post-its had vanished. There was nothing on the desk but the computer, the printer, and a photograph of the family in a silver frame. 'She's finished her new book already. That must be why she's seeing the Dreaditor – to give it to her.'

That was it, then. The final end to the *Mermaid Girls*, undeniable at last.

Pea took a deep breath, and brushed her sadness aside. She was mature. She was sophisticated.

And there was more important work to do.

'What are we looking for now?' asked Tinkerbell as Pea turned on the computer with sweaty hands.

She typed slowly, her heart in her mouth.

Nothing came up for *Belvedeke Hotel* – but there were links to various *Belvedere Hotels*. Heart pounding, Pea clicked on the first one, which was in London.

There was a map, and a photograph, and a link to which tube station was nearest. The Belvedere Hotel was less than half an hour away from their own raspberry-red front door.

And tomorrow, at eleven o'clock, Ewan McGregor would be there, waiting for her.

CHAPTER

10

THE BELVEDERE HOTEL

It took two minutes on Mum's computer, a quick discussion with a beaming Tinkerbell, and a solemn conversation over the garden wall with both of the Sams, while Surprise ran noisily around the puppy-training obstacle course.

Nose promises were made to keep it all a secret, even from Clover. (Pea took most promises seriously, but nose promises – spoken with a finger pressed to the end of the nose – were meant to be unbreakable.)

Then Pea went back inside, and giddily took up her pen.

Dear Dad,

I got your secret message!

We've made a plan. Sam Two helped. She's bad at keeping secrets but brilliant at plans so I decided it was worth the risk.

I will be at the hotel at exactly the right time. (I hope. Your secret message was a bit rubbish. If it is 11 o'clock at night then that's past my bedtime, but I expect you've thought of that.)

I am too excited to go to sleep!!!

Lots and lots and lots of love from Pea xx

By the time Pea made it downstairs for breakfast on Saturday morning, the plan was already being set up.

'Can we go into London while Clover's at slug rehearsals?' Tinkerbell was asking. 'Pea and me? We've got urgent secret birthday shopping to do.'

Clover flashed Pea a smile, obviously pleased she was taking her advice about Mum's present.

Pea blushed as she put jam on her toast. Clover would understand, once the plan had happened, and Ewan McGregor was right there in front of them, in all his spy/pirate/rock-climbing glory.

'I don't see why not,' said Mum, and giggled. 'In fact, that's a gorgeous idea, my chicks. I've been working boringly hard. I deserve a day out with my baby girls.'

Pea remembered the Dreaditor meeting and the empty desk – but there was too much excitement bubbling in her stomach for any gloominess to last.

'You can't come, though, Mum,' said Tinkerbell. 'Because it's secret birthday shopping for you.'

Mum folded her arms. 'I know you're eight now, which is *extremely* grown-up – but I'm still not sending you two off to go shopping by yourselves. Not in central London.'

The phone rang.

It was Dr Paget. *Apparently*, Dr Skidelsky was going to take the twins into the city to test Surprise's new good behaviour in a real-world environment. *Apparently*, she was wondering if Pea and Tinkerbell might like to come along.

'What a coincidence!' said Pea, in an awkward high-pitched voice.

Tinkerbell kicked her under the table.

But Mum was too busy chatting on the phone to notice. When she hung up, she smiled. 'Well, I'll look forward to spending a lovely *evening* with my baby girls, instead. That's fairer to Clover, after all.'

And that settled it. Dr Skidelsky would call round in fifteen minutes to take them into town. Clover would go to her rehearsal. Mum and Dr Paget could go out for a lazy lunch later. And Noelle could be left in peace to sleep in before her next English lesson.

They heard the Paget-Skidelskys arriving long before the doorbell rang. Surprise was making a

low, howling, growling noise – possibly prompted
by the mysterious bulge in Sam Two's coat pocket,
or perhaps by the paper sign taped onto his tartan
dog jacket: PUPPY IN TRAINING.

'We won't come in, don't worry!' shouted Dr
Skidelsky over Wuffly's barks when Pea opened the
front door.

Sam One gave her a shy smile, and secretly
unfolded a piece of paper from his pocket: a hand-
drawn map of the Thames, with the Belvedere
Hotel clearly marked.

Pea beamed back. 'What's that?' she whispered,
pointing at a strange hoop drawn beside the river,
with lots of small dots around its edge.

'The London Eye,' Sam One whispered back.
'The big wheel? Your dad's hotel is practically next
door.'

Pea felt her stomach flip over. If she had to pick
a hotel in London, she'd want one that had a view
of a big wheel too.

Mum and Clover waved them off.

'Are we sure this is a good idea?' said Dr Skidelsky, rearing back as Surprise strained on his lead and began to drag Sam Two along the pavement.

'It's a brilliant idea!' said Tinkerbell. 'Dogs only learn from experience, just like people. Wuffly used to be a bit bitey with strangers, but after she'd chomped on twenty or so she got the hang of them.'

'Mm,' said Dr Skidelsky, not looking reassured.

'You've got a handful there!' said a cheery man in uniform, giving Dr Skidelsky a wink as he opened up the extra-wide-luggage gates to let them all through.

Pea wasn't sure if he meant the puppy or the four children, one of whom was wearing a top hat and an eyeliner moustache. From Dr Skidelsky's weak smile, neither was she. Surprise frantically snuffled at every bench, blob of sticky chewing gum or passing shoe on Queen's Park platform, but once they were on the train and in a dark tunnel, he calmed down. He sat quietly on Sam Two's lap, nosing at her strangely bulging coat pocket, while

Sam Two said, 'Sit,' and 'Good dog,' and stroked him. Every time the train stopped and the doors opened up with a beep, his ears pricked up and he wagged his tail as if that was their stop, but Pea thought no one could blame him for that; every time she went on the tube she was just the same, worrying that she might get off at the wrong station.

They took the Bakerloo Line all the way to Waterloo, then walked towards the river.

It was a sunny day; cool enough to still need a coat, but with a bright blue sky and the fluffy sort of clouds. The South Bank was teeming with families and tourists soaking up the first hints of summer. There were brightly coloured lights strung up in the trees, street jugglers and human statues, stalls selling fresh juice and roast pork sandwiches. Surprise wanted to sniff out every inch. It made their progress achingly slow – and every time the puppy knotted his lead around a stranger's ankles, Dr Skidelsky had to stop and apologize, with frantic pointing at the PUPPY IN TRAINING sign.

When she spotted a shiny silver van selling coffee and fresh doughnuts, she looked desperately relieved. 'Triple espresso, please! And – doughnut for everyone?'

Pea shook her head. She couldn't eat now, not when her insides were so squirmy with anticipation. But the other three all nodded eagerly.

'It's only ten forty,' whispered Sam Two, surreptitiously checking her watch. 'That's bags of time.'

'And all this secret planning needs lots of energy,' added Tinkerbell, her nose covered in sugar.

Once Dr Skidelsky had 'refuelled', they set off again, this time with Sam One holding the lead. Pea could see the loop of the London Eye now. She drifted through the crowds in a daze. Her heart thumped unsteadily in her chest. Dr Skidelsky asked her a question about school, and Pea's mouth answered it automatically, without her brain joining in at all. It was already trained exclusively on the big white wheel, and the looming building beside it; the one with the rows and rows of windows, like a hotel . . .

The London Eye drew so close they were only a few steps from the end of the queue, and could see the faces of the people in the pods, slowly lifting into the air to see the view.

Sam Two checked her watch. 'Ten fifty-five,' she whispered.

Tinkerbell slipped her hand into Pea's and gave it a little squeeze. 'Ready?' she asked in a whisper.

Pea swallowed hard, and nodded.

With a grin, Sam Two dipped her hand into her bulgy pocket, produced something small and orange, and hurled it into the queue for the London Eye.

Tinkerbell let go of Pea's hand.

Sam One let go of the puppy's lead.

With a yelp and a terrific burst of speed, Surprise bounded after his beloved carrot.

'Stop! No! *Puppy!*' yelled Dr Skidelsky.

The queue of people scattered in alarm as Surprise hurled himself into the forest of ankles,

trailing his lead. Sam Two sprinted after him, disappearing into the crowd, Tinkerbell on her heels.

'No, girls – wait—' cried Dr Skidelsky, taking
one step towards them, then hanging back to throw
a panicky look at Pea and Sam One.

'We'll stay right here,' said Sam One, on cue.
'We'll go and sit on that bench, over there, and we
won't move till you come back.'

'Yes. Good. Thank goodness I've got two sensible
ones, at least,' breathed Dr Skidelsky. Then she
plunged into the queue, declaring, 'Sorry . . . sorry
. . . No, sir, I'm really not trying to push in, I assure
you . . . Have you seen two girls and a small dog?'

Within seconds she was lost in the crowd.

Pea stood breathless, frozen to the spot as the
big wheel turned against the blue sky, and the tourists went on by. Here she was, out in the middle of
London, very nearly by herself, to meet her father
for the very first time. She knew she was meant
to be mature and sophisticated now, but it was
suddenly overwhelming.

'Are we going, then?' asked Sam One.

Once he was holding out the map, she felt calmer. With a quick look behind them at the disarray in the queue for the Eye, they ran alongside a park, until they came to a road. It was full of cars, taxis beeping their horns, and one stinky bin lorry – but once that drove off, Pea could see the sign on the wall opposite.

BELVEDERE ROAD.

When she spun round, there it was. A purple canopy sticking out above a stone staircase, with a crest and *Belvedere Hotel* printed on it in grand curling white letters.

Pea broke into a run. There were two sets of double doors with brass handles, and then they were inside.

It was hushed compared to the noisy chaos of the London street, and much too warm, as if they had suddenly plunged underwater. A large wood-panelled room opened up to their right, with a long high counter like at a bank only without the glass screens. A sign hanging above it said RECEPTION. To their left was a small café area, with round tables and plush purple armchairs. There were two people drinking cups of coffee and having a whispery conversation – perhaps the sort that spies having a secret meeting might have? – and Pea peered at them hopefully. But one was a young woman wearing a purple uniform that matched the chairs, with blue streaks in her hair and a nose-ring. The other had her back to Pea, a bright red scarf looped around her head – definitely a woman too.

There was no sign of a big-chinned, red-bearded American.

There were no other children there, either.

Pea suddenly felt enormously self-conscious.

'What now?' whispered Sam One.

Pea looked at the big clock on the wall behind the reception desk.

11.02.

'I suppose we could ask which room he's staying in,' she whispered.

A young man with tufty blond hair and a purple tie beckoned them over.

The reception desk was so high up, Pea could barely rest her chin on it, and the man with the purple tie had to stand up to see her.

'Good morning, welcome to the Belvedere Hotel, my name is Simon, how may I help you today?' he said, in a singsongy rush, as if he'd said it a hundred times before.

'I'm looking for a, um, family member who's staying here, I think. He's expecting us, so I wondered if you could call his room, or maybe tell us which number he's in.'

'What's the name?'

'Ewan McGregor.'

Simon had begun typing into his computer, but he stopped at once, and glared at Pea. 'That's not very funny, little girl,' he said.

'She's not a little girl, she'll be twelve next week,' said Sam One. 'And that *is* his name, honestly.'

'It *is*,' said Pea in a small voice.

Simon pursed his lips, but he typed it in all the same. Then he pursed his lips even more, and leaned over the desk. 'Someone told you to come and wind me up, yeah?' he said, in what was probably a normal speaking voice, but in the hushed reception of the Belvedere Hotel sounded like a shout. 'Well, I'm not laughing. Leave now, before I call security.'

Pea could feel eyes turning her way. The blue-haired woman and the woman with her head wrapped in the red scarf began to talk rapidly, and jiggle their coffee cups.

'Maybe he's not actually staying here,' she said, standing on tiptoe and tipping her chin up. 'Do you have a meeting room? Like, do people come here for special appointments? Because I have a special appointment . . .' She reached into her pocket for the envelope, and showed him the back of the letter.

'It says Saturday, at eleven,' she explained helpfully.

'If you say so,' said Simon, pushing it back across the desk with a curl of his lip. 'But no, we don't have meeting rooms. Just the café.'

'I don't understand . . .' Pea whispered, staring at the letter.

Sam One took the envelope from her, and studied it closely, running his thumb over the stamp. He handed it back to her with a strange expression on his face. 'You know that there isn't even a postmark?' he said slowly. 'I don't think this letter was posted at all. Someone only wanted you to think it was.'

'But then how did it get to my house?'

'Well . . .' said Sam One, blinking at her reluctantly. 'Maybe it was written there?'

Pea's insides flipped over.

With an awful feeling of dread, she added it all up.

The locked study.

The mysterious refusal to discuss Greek islands.

Mums know everything . . . Maybe even what

was written in letters, and tucked away in a bedside drawer?

Suddenly the hotel hush was shattered by a crash of double doors. Bursting through them came Mum, her face streaked with tears, Dr Paget panting after her.

'Pea! Oh, my starling, what on earth did you think you were— Oh, I don't know whether to shake you or kiss you!'

She swept towards Pea and whirled her into a hug that lifted her right off the floor. Pea felt a long kiss being pressed onto the top of her head. Then Mum let go and stepped back, still keeping hold of Pea's shoulders.

'Are you all right?'

Pea nodded dizzily.

'And Sam?'

Sam One was fiddling with his jumper cuffs, and shrugging under Dr Paget's gaze.

'No, wait . . .' Pea looked into her mum's red-rimmed eyes. 'I'm *not* all right. It was you all along, wasn't it? You're E M. You sent the letter.'

Mum drew herself up to her full height, took a deep breath, and said quite calmly and clearly, 'No. I didn't. But I know who did.'

There was another clatter of coffee cups from the café. When Pea turned to look, the blue-haired woman was edging out towards the counter. The woman in the red scarf was shrinking away, as if trying to disappear into the table. In her hands was a box; a square box wrapped in shiny paper, with a bow on the top.

A birthday present.

Pea took a tentative step forward, confused.

The woman tugged the red scarf off. Familiar stringy curtains of hair appeared, framing a long bony nose.

Noelle.

CHAPTER
11

E M

'I sorry! I sorry!' wailed Noelle.

'I should hope so!' shouted Mum.

Pea quivered all over. She'd never seen Mum looking so angry in her whole life.

'But,' said Pea, looking bewilderedly from one to the other, 'I don't understand. *How* could Noelle have written the letter?'

'That's kind of my fault,' said a nervy voice with an American accent. The blue-haired girl rippled the fingers of one hand in an rueful wave. 'Hey. I'm Tansy. Klaudia's friend? I've been teaching Noelle some English, and—'

'I explain!' wept Noelle through her hair. 'It is the photographs, and the family sad, and the homesick! I am having very unhappy for this poor Pea and no papa, and I am telling Tansy, and I am telling her also of these letters – letters never to send?'

'Make-it-Better Letters,' murmured Dr Paget.

'And I am telling Tansy how I am finding a letter in the furniture of Pea, to her papa. It is sad! We are both of crying! We think to write a letter, to be kind, to be happy. Tansy, she perform the writings, so it is the good English words. I am thinking, the papa will disappear like magic trick, *pouf*. It work! This Pea, she is so happy.'

Pea stared. Noelle had seemed so wrapped up in her own miserableness that Pea had never imagined she cared.

'But then I find a letter new from Pea, very sad. She wish this papa does not write to her, oui? She very sad. I very sad. I am thinking, Ah! It goes bad. I must make end, I must make it forget.'

Pea remembered the sobbing in the kitchen, the stiff one-armed-hug, and began to understand.

'Today, I have the lesson with Tansy, here, in this hotel—'

'I work here at weekends,' said Tansy, rippling her fingers again.

'*Oui*, yes, we meet here – but when I am waking up, I am seeing a new letter, and this Belvedere Hotel, ah! So I am thinking: the Pea, she wants *un cadeau d'anniversaire* from her papa. I buy *le cadeau*, Tansy she write letter, papa he goes pouf, everyone has happy, everyone forget. But – you are here. I am too late.' She broke off at last, and blew her nose loudly.

Pea stood very still, and wondered if she might be sick, right there, on the shiny floor of the Belvedere Hotel.

'How did you find us?' asked Sam One, looking nervously up at Dr Paget.

Mum smiled weakly. 'Because, Sam, when Pea looks up a hotel in London on my computer, and

232

when you look up a map to that hotel in London on yours, me and your Mum Gen don't have too much trouble putting it all together. And then there were Pea's letters.'

Pea quivered. 'So you read them? Everything I wrote to – to Ewan McGregor?'

Noelle made a small whimpery noise.

'I read enough,' said Mum. 'Enough to understand that you'd been writing to someone you thought was your dad. Of course I was *horrified* at you running off to meet some stranger, so I went straight to Noelle's room to ask if you'd told her about any of it. She'd already gone out, but there on the bed was her diary, with today's lesson marked in it: eleven a.m. at the Belvedere Hotel, just like your map.'

'You can forgive?' sniffled Noelle. 'I so sorry. Forgive?'

'Um,' said Pea, looking at Mum for some sort of guidance.

'We were trying to be nice, I swear it,' added Tansy.

Mum made a low growling noise.

'Let's worry about that later, shall we?' said Dr Paget, in a bright voice. 'I think that nice young man in the purple tie might like us to stop arguing in the middle of his hotel, and we probably ought to go and find the rest of them.'

Mum gasped. 'Tink! And the others! Oh no – what have you done to poor Kara?'

Sam One began to explain, but Pea decided it would be quicker to show them.

They all hurried out, and she led them through the crowds till they were back beside the river, sunshine bouncing off the slow-moving pods of the London Eye.

Dr Skidelsky was easy to spot, standing with her hands on her hips and her oblong glasses slipping down her nose as she shielded her eyes from the bright sun. Sam Two was sitting a few metres away on the bench where she and Sam One had promised to wait, with the sulky expression of someone who has been told off, loudly, in a public place.

'Oh, thank goodness,' breathed Dr Skidelsky on seeing them. 'I've been trying to call you, ever since I managed to drag a confession out of this one.'

Sam Two looked even more sulky.

'But where's Tinkerbell? And the puppy?'

Pea shielded her eyes and pointed up at the Eye. Most of the pods had ten or twelve people inside – tiny from the ground but close enough to easily tell them apart – all standing sensibly still and taking pictures of the view. But in one pod, nearing the top, there seemed to be a hurricane. A tiny, hairy, grey hurricane, accompanied by a small brown girl in a top hat.

'Oh no,' whispered Mum.

'Oh wow,' said Sam One.

'I know!' said Sam Two, sulkiness replaced by a proud grin. 'I never thought she'd actually make it inside.'

As they watched, the hurricane bounded from one end of the pod to the other, bounced off the glass, and launched himself at an old man (who tried to fight him off with his newspaper: the newspaper did not come off well in the encounter). Eventually the small brown girl leaped across the pod, and lay on top of the hurricane. It was surprisingly effective. Pea could see the people inside the pod applauding. Apparently, lots of the crowd below were watching, and they clapped too. Sam Two joined in, until a look from Dr Skidelsky made her meekly put her hands in her pockets.

Back in the pod, the girl got up to take a bow – and the hurricane began again, to groans and giggles from the crowd.

By the time the slow wheel had turned all the way round and dropped Tinkerbell and Surprise back to earth, the Paget-Skidelskys had been to the manager's office to explain, and pay for her ticket.

'Oh!' said Tinkerbell when she saw Mum standing there. She peered at the group, then at Pea. 'Did, um, Peter Rabbit not turn up then?'

Pea shook her head quickly.

'Never mind all that! Tinkerbell Louisa Llewellyn, what on earth did you think you were doing?'

'It was easy, really. The pods keep on going round and round without stopping, so I just threw the carrot in at the right time, let go of the lead, and followed Surprise in before they could stop me. But he didn't bite anyone!' Tinkerbell patted Surprise's head as he danced around Dr Paget's ankles. 'He was naughty for some bits, but then, he's a dog and he's never been in the sky before, and it is a bit strange being all high up. He didn't wee anywhere, either. But when he got bored with his carrot he did eat my hat.'

Crestfallen, she held out the top hat. The brim and part of the crown were very chewed, and the satin ribbon had come off.

'I think that's the very least punishment you deserve,' said Mum severely. Then she gave Tinkerbell a hug that lasted quite a long time, before telling her off again.

'I'm hungry. Can we have another doughnut?' asked Sam Two.

'No!' chorused Dr Paget, Dr Skidelsky and Mum, all at once.

'Can we have noodles?'

'No!' came the chorus again.

'Although,' said Dr Paget guiltily, 'we did say we were going out for lunch, and it *is* a lovely sunny day . . .'

Noelle was despatched to take Surprise home, and they ordered spicy noodles to share at an outdoor table, watching the world go by.

Pea blinked up at the sky, blue and bright, spotted with fluffy clouds. That it was the same sky from only an hour before, when she was so excited to meet her dad – who missed her and loved her and had said *I am so sorry* – seemed quite impossible. She felt hollowed out, ghostly, as if she were not quite real. *And* there were prawns in her noodles.

But she ate them anyway.

❀ ❀ ❀

Clover crashed through the raspberry-red front door just after four.

'You look exactly how I feel,' she sighed, flopping down on the red sofa next to Pea. 'I've tried and tried to tell Marko, but I'm still a grey slug for almost all of the play.'

Once Tinkerbell had explained about Noelle, even Clover conceded that Pea won at upsetness today – though she was appalled at them keeping it a secret.

'Why didn't you tell me? I would've told you it was a terrible plan!'

'Exactly!' said Tinkerbell.

A familiar sniffling sound wafted down the hallway. Then Mum poked her head round the door.

'Family meeting, my ducks, in the kitchen.'

Pea felt nervous. They'd never had an official family meeting before; usually things just sorted themselves out with ordinary talking.

Noelle was sitting at the kitchen table, a box of tissues at the ready.

They all sat down. Wuffly curled up at Tinkerbell's feet.

'Now,' said Mum, 'first things first: you're all in complete disgrace for making secret plans and running off into London— No, Clover, it's not interrupting time. But before we get to that: I've had a little chat with Noelle, and we've agreed that really, even before all this happened, she wasn't very happy. In fact, I think it was missing her own father that made her do such a foolish thing, hmm?'

Noelle nodded miserably.

'I've spoken to her family, and we've agreed that being an *au pair* isn't quite the right job for her; at least for now. She's going back to France in a few days to do some more studying, and perhaps a little bit more growing up too.'

There was an awkward silence.

'Do we have to pretend to be sad?' whispered Tinkerbell, in Pea's ear.

Pea gave her a jab with an elbow. She *was* sad – but in a complicated sort of way.

'We're very sorry you didn't enjoy living here more, and we hope being at home cheers you up,' said Clover.

It was – once 'cheer you up' had been translated for Noelle – the perfect thing to say.

'And was there something you wanted to say to the girls, Noelle?'

Noelle coughed, then spoke in her whisper-quiet voice.

'I sorry for not being better with the English, and the homework, and the fun games. You are beautiful, kind girls. And to Pea: I sorry for the letter. Tansy is also sorry, but the fault, it is mine. I have big big sorry. I am hoping you can forgive.'

Pea shuffled her shoulders. 'I think so.'

'Thank you, thank you!'

'But don't do that to someone again, will you? Because . . .' Pea frowned. 'I see that you wanted to be kind, but it was unkind, really. You made me hope. And if we hadn't found you at the hotel, I would've gone on thinking it was real, when it never was, and that's not kind either.'

Mum made a small sound, between a sigh and a sob, and covered her mouth with her hand.

'Of course, of course,' whispered Noelle, bobbing her head.

Then she reached under the table and produced the present she had been clutching in the café of the Belvedere Hotel.

'Alas, it is not *un cadeau d'anniversaire* from your papa. Perhaps you will accept *un cadeau d'apologie*. From me. To say sorry.'

Pea read the tag.

> To Pea
> Happy Birthday from your father
> E M xx

She put it down again, and looked plaintively at Mum. To Pea's great relief, she plucked the box off the table and tucked it away out of sight.

'We'll worry about that later, shall we? Now, Noelle – would you mind going away? I need to talk to my girls.'

Taking three tissues from the box to keep her going, Noelle sniffled her way back into her little private room, and shut the door.

'Now,' said Mum, looking very solemn.

'We're completely hugely totally sorry,' said Tinkerbell rapidly.

Pea nodded. 'I am, I promise. I don't know how it happened, even.'

'It all started because of Granny Duff, and my watch, and not wanting to miss out on family things,' said Clover. 'So we had very good intentions – at the beginning. I mean, I didn't do any of the really awful part. But it got a bit out of control.'

'And we do know going off to a hotel to meet someone we don't know at all is very wrong,' added Pea. 'And lying about going into London. And running off from Dr Skidelsky. And sneaking onto the London Eye with a puppy.'

'Though I am the youngest, and Pea should've stopped me, so it's a bit more her fault than mine,' added Tinkerbell. 'What? It's true!'

'Have you finished? Good,' said Mum. 'I'm glad you said all that, because now I don't have to – although how you managed to know all that and still go off and . . . But then, we all do things we know aren't right, I suppose. In fact, that's what I need to talk to you about, my swans. This family meeting isn't just so I can tell you off. I think you might want to tell *me* off too, once I've told you the truth – and you'll be quite entitled.'

She gave another heavy sigh, and plucked a tissue from the box. To Pea's astonishment, her hand was shaking.

'Pea, my darling girl, your father isn't quite what you think – what I *let* you think all this time. I *did* meet him on a Greek island while I was working there, and he *was* an American. But the rest . . . I didn't know him for very long, just a few weeks. We didn't plan to have a baby. By the time I found out you were on the way, he'd already gone back to America.'

Pea shook her head firmly. 'No, Mum, that can't be right. He was there when I was born. He was there in the hospital to give me my name. Then he disappeared into the night and was never heard from again. That's what happened, Mum.'

Pea wasn't sure why she needed the old familiar story to stay true, or why it cracked her heart so much when Mum shook her head.

'I'm so sorry, my baby.' She reached her hand across the table to cover Pea's. 'That – that didn't happen. I hoped it would. That's why I stayed in Cephalonia. It takes nine long months to grow a baby, you know. I stayed, and I wrote to him, but he never wrote back, and he wasn't at the hospital. The nurses named you, after the song that was playing on the radio, *Dear Prudence* – and once you had a name, it seemed like bad luck to choose another.'

'Like with a boat?' said Tinkerbell.

Mum laughed, giving her a surprised look. 'Yes,

that's what they say, isn't it? Maybe that's what I was thinking of. Like with a boat.'

So the one thing Pea's father had chosen for her had been given by strangers, after all.

'He liked it, though, that you were named after a Beatles song,' said Mum.

'What?' said Pea, confused. 'When?'

'After The Flood. I'd told him about you, of course, sent him a few baby pictures, but it only made me miserable when he didn't answer. But when all the passports got ruined, I thought it was important to give him another chance.'

Pea's heart leaped. 'Clover said! She said you'd tried to find him – only you couldn't, because of all the moving around, and him being called Ewan McGregor.'

Mum looked embarrassed. 'Oh, my chick. I *did* find him – but he still wasn't interested in being part of our little family. And, er, his name isn't Ewan McGregor.'

'What?' yelped Clover.

'I'm sorry! I know. Evan Magruder – that's your father's name. Clover, you knew that, once upon a time, you've just forgotten. One day you called him Ewan McGregor – I think you'd seen his name on a film poster – and since it was funny, I never corrected it. Him being there on the night you were born – I think that was me, telling a story to comfort us both. The piratical flit in the moonlight? I think it came about naturally, to explain why he was gone if he'd been there that night. Same for your name. As the years went by, the story grew and grew, until it became such a good story that everyone believed it. Even me, a little bit. And it was a cheerfuller story than the real one, so I let it happen, and I promised myself that when you were ready, Pea-nut, I'd tell you the truth. Only I missed that moment, and now you're old enough to be upset, and angry, and rightly so.'

Mum stroked the back of Pea's hand with her fingertip. 'What you said to Noelle earlier,' she said, in a croaky voice, 'about how it *was* unkind to let you hope; that was perfectly true. And that's what I did. I let you hope, and it was unkind. I'm so very sorry. So sorry to you all.'

Pea felt very odd. She'd heard Mum say sorry lots of times before – for the Well-Behaved times, when a winter coat being forgotten on a bus meant extra jumpers squashed under the summer one until next year, and when they were forever arriving in a new place or leaving it behind. It wasn't always easy, and it definitely wasn't always fun. But they'd done it together. This was something else: a secret kept on purpose. A secret about her.

'Wow,' said Tinkerbell. 'That's worse than anything I've done, ever. Even that time I put toast in the DVD player.'

'Much worse,' said Mum, giggling in that sniffly way people have when they're upset but desperately don't want to be.

'Do you really want us to tell you off?' asked Clover, in a faint voice.

'Not really. I'd like you to forgive me, more than

anything, but I know that might take a long time. You might never. But maybe you could all try to be very grown-up about it, and if you can't quite forgive me, you could understand instead. It was a mistake, to make you believe something that wasn't true. But – well, like Noelle and her letter, I promise you I never, ever meant to hurt any of you. Just the opposite. Are you all right, Pea? You're very quiet.'

Pea thought she ought to be cross; furious even. Or sobbing. But she felt curiously calm and thoughtful. Perhaps it was proof that she really *was* growing up, after all; being mature and sophisticated about shocking news, instead of stamping her foot or bursting into tears.

But Mum was a grown-up, and she'd fibbed and messed up and made mistakes; was still making them, even now. Noelle was eighteen, and Mum had said she needed to grow up too.

Pea thought that perhaps being grown up wasn't such a big change after all. An adult could do something childish, or wrong, just like *she* might.

They weren't completely sewn-together people. They might sometimes be quite like children. And somehow, in amongst all her disappointment, she felt a tiny bit relieved.

'Well?' said Mum, squeezing her hand.

'I'm sort of horribly sad,' said Pea, 'but I think I understand, a bit. Thank you for telling me the truth.'

There were hugs, and Mum and Clover made cups of tea.

'What do we do with this?' asked Clover, lifting the shiny parcel with the bow on top back onto the table.

To Pea
Happy Birthday from your father
E M xx

Pea looked at the box. It was square – the wrong shape to have a bra or a book in; too big for a watch. She couldn't imagine what might be inside.

She picked up the box and pressed it close to

her heart, almost as if she were giving it a hug. Then she put it back down on the table and pushed it away.

'I think it should stay wrapped up,' she said slowly. 'I liked my real dad better when he was a pirate called Ewan McGregor who played *Dear Prudence* on the guitar, and now we've unwrapped the real him, that's all gone. So I don't want to open it ever, and then I can imagine it's something brilliant. Does that make sense?'

'Lots,' said Mum, and put it away in a cupboard.

Late that night, just as she was falling asleep, there was a tapping at her bedroom door.

'Pea?' whispered Tinkerbell, into the darkness. 'Will we have to call you Pea Magruder now?'

'No!' Pea whispered back. 'Now go to sleep!'

No, she was still Pea Llewellyn, just like always.

CHAPTER 12

HAPPY BIRTHDAY, PEA

One week later, it was Saturday again – 28th May.

Mum's birthday.

Pea's birthday.

Pea set her alarm clock to go off just before seven, so that she could have a few minutes of getting used to being twelve before Tinkerbell let Wuffly in to leap on her bed.

Twelve, it turned out, felt a lot like eleven.

She had the tingly excitement of a birthday, sure enough – especially since she had no idea what to expect from her surprise party – but she didn't feel changed. Her legs didn't seem longer. There was no urgent desire to listen to the morning news on Radio 4, or read a magazine about which trousers were best. She got out of bed to look in the bathroom mirror, just to check, but the pale freckly face reflected back to her looked exactly the same as yesterday's.

'Let me carry it,' came a loud whisper from downstairs, along with the smell of burning toast.

'No! It's heavy and there's hot things and you've nearly ruined everything already.' That was definitely Clover. 'You can bring the mugs – they won't fit on the tray.'

Mum wandered out of her bedroom, yawning, her hair in a big tumbly mess around her head. She was frowning at the burned smell, but when she spotted Pea, her face lit up.

'Happy birthday, Pea-pod,' she said softly, and gave her a hug.

'Happy birthday to you too,' said Pea, hugging back.

'Shh! You'll wake them up and ruin the surprise!'

Clover's voice echoed up from below, along with the clinking of glass and china.

Mum grinned at Pea, and put her finger to her lips to mean *Shh!* – and they both tiptoed back to bed.

When, a few minutes later, Pea's door was knocked and her bed bounced on by a very excitable dog, she produced a perfectly convincing fake yawn. Tinkerbell shooed her and Wuffly down the attic steps and into Mum's room, where both she and Mum claimed sincere surprise at the arrival of their breakfast in bed, and said 'Happy birthday' to each other all over again.

The breakfast was weak tea, and black toast which had been sliced up and glued to plates with strawberry jam so that it spelled out HAPPY BIRTHDAY – or near enough.

'There were eggs, but now there aren't,' explained Tinkerbell.

'They were meant to spell out PEA and MUM,' added Clover, 'but apparently making eggs spell words just makes nasty eggs.'

'The fact that you tried is lovely enough,' said Mum, scraping the black bits off the letter B. 'Now, Tink, stick your nose under the bed, will you? Because I think you'll find a few unwrappable things under there . . .'

Pea wriggled with excitement as a small pile of presents appeared. 'Did you fetch . . . ?' she whispered – but Clover nodded, and put one round, humped, very loosely wrapped present off to one side.

'You first,' said Mum, nudging Pea.

They took turns, with Tinkerbell acting as Head Bin Operative, and scrunching up all the paper and tags into a ball.

Pea got a handmade clay pencil topper from Tinkerbell, in the shape of a horrible monster with teeth. Mum had one too, but hers had tentacles instead.

'To scare you both into writing faster,' Tinkerbell explained.

Clover gave Pea a new notebook with a beautiful

pattern on the front like a stained-glass window, and a little ribbon attached to the spine which tucked inside to keep your place.

'Oh, that's lovely!' said Mum, stroking the stained glass pattern. 'Perfect to replace that one you lost, don't you think?'

Pea nodded, stroking the cover too.

Next Mum unwrapped a necklace from Clover: turquoise, with tiny golden leaves hanging off it. She put it on at once.

Pea's last present was from Clem; a tiny square wrapped in golden paper, so light it felt as if there was nothing inside – which there wasn't; only a cardboard gift tag that said *See you later, Birthday Girl! xxx*

'He's coming to my party?' asked Pea.

Mum nodded, smiling. 'He said he couldn't miss it – or your play, Alice, slugs or no slugs.'

Pea felt warm all over. It was lovely. It was exactly what she wanted – but she hadn't expected it to be her last present. She quietly hunted around the folds of the duvet as if she were rearranging it, looking for her other present, her best, the one from Mum – but Mum was already being handed the humpy blob of wrapping paper.

'I hope it's all right,' said Pea, suddenly nervous.

She'd found it very hard to pick a present for Mum this year. Noelle had been waved off in a taxi to the airport on Tuesday, so she couldn't take Pea to the shops. She'd tried various crafty projects – but her knitting was holey, and her origami frog necklace looked like paper and string and not like a necklace at all. Dr Paget had come to her rescue yesterday after school, taking a weepy Pea to her plush golden sofa and listening to her thoughtfully, as if Pea were one of her therapy patients. They had talked for nearly half an hour, not only about birthdays, and by the end of it Pea felt more than ever that she wanted to give Mum a really good present this year.

The result had been made last night, with

creative assistance from the Sams, and collected by Clover in secret.

'There's only paper on the top half,' explained Pea, when Mum looked surprised to be holding a plate. Once she unpeeled the sticky tape, Mum pulled back the stripy paper to reveal a cake decorated with a portrait of Mum made from dribbles of icing, sprinkles, and spun sugar for hair – golden threads that stuck up above the cake and made a sort of wiry cloud around her face.

'Dr Paget did the spun sugar, because it's burning hot,' said Pea. 'And Sam One helped with making it look more like you. But I cooked the cake and did all the rest. I thought we've always shared a cake on our birthday, and you never have one that's all for you – so that's your present. A Mum cake. Happy birthday.'

Mum gave the cake – and Pea – a round of applause, and declared that it was a very good thing the eggs had turned out nasty and the toast was a bit burned, as that way they all had an excuse to have cake for breakfast.

'No, it's your cake, for you!' protested Pea.

But Mum said that meant she got to decide who had some, which seemed fair enough.

'I might be too nervy for cake,' said Clover, looking wan at the prospect of her first perform-ance as Alice that night. 'Even being a grey slug brings on stage-fright, you know.' But somehow, once she'd had one bite, the rest of her slice disap-peared easily enough.

Pea's slice had one dolly-mixture eye, which she picked off and saved for last.

Tinkerbell sucked on some spun-sugar hair, then frowned. 'Hang on. Where's Pea's present from Mum?'

Mum licked her fingers, and smiled. 'An excellent question. I think Pea might have been wondering that herself, even if she was too polite to say so. But you'll have to be patient a little longer, Pea-nut. There will be a delivery later today, so when you hear the doorbell, that's when you'll get your present. And no, I can't tell you anything about your party yet, either.'

'But you're still coming to my play, aren't you?' asked Clover, looking frantic.

'Of course,' said Mum. 'You'll see.'

And she hopped out of bed, kissed them all, and took the rest of the Mum cake downstairs so they wouldn't be tempted.

Pea ate the rest of her cake in such a state of curiosity she barely tasted it.

'What did you ask for?' demanded Tinkerbell. 'You must know.'

'I don't. Did she really not tell you?'

'Not a thing,' said Clover. 'I saw her writing invitations, but she hid them. And she hasn't asked us to do any decorating or party cooking or anything.'

It didn't sound like a usual sort of Llewellyn birthday party, then. It wouldn't be like Clover's, or Tinkerbell's. Pea had no idea at all what to expect.

Even when she ran downstairs to ask what sort of clothes she ought to wear, Mum said, 'Oh, birthday party clothes, of course,' which gave nothing whatsoever away.

It was thrilling.

The morning hours ticked by astonishingly slowly.

Clover locked herself in the bathroom for an hour and a half for 'pre-opening-night exfoliation. If I have to be a slug, I might as well be a slug with peachy skin.'

Tinkerbell put on her chewed top hat and her cumberbatch, and distracted Pea with a new version of Find the Lady. There were still three cups to choose from, but instead of guessing which one had a ball underneath, you had to guess which hid one of Wuffly's doggy drops – while Wuffly ran around the cups barking in addled fascination.

The doorbell rang just after ten – but it was only the post lady, bringing a few cards for them both.

'Oh dear, have I made it too exciting?' asked Mum as Pea's shoulders slumped. 'It'll be another hour or so to wait, my lambs. But worth it, I promise.'

They took Wuffly for a walk.

Pea stuck all the birthday cards on the fridge door.

She even sat briefly on Mum's chair in the study, staring at the computer screen and wondering what would happen if she typed in *Evan Magruder*. But instead she went upstairs, put the toothy monster on the end of her pen, and opened her new notebook from Clover. She scratched her nose with one of the monster's pointy ears, and pondered a new story; one about a birthday.

She was still trying to think of a good name for her main character when there was a yell from downstairs.

'Door! Door!' howled Tinkerbell.

'But my hair's not finished!' wailed Clover, who emerged onto the landing with her straighteners in her hand, one half of her long blonde hair its usual tumbly fluffy self, the other poker-straight.

'No one cares,' yelled Mum. 'Now, where's the birthday girl to open this door?'

Pea almost tripped, she was so desperate to get down the stairs. The front door was still closed, and whoever was outside rang the bell *and* knocked, as if they were getting impatient.

Tinkerbell and Mum were lined up in the hallway, waiting. Clover sat on the bottom of the stairs, now wearing a bobble-hat to hide the lopsided hair.

'Go on,' hissed Mum, a twinkle in her eye.

Pea reached up, twisted the lock, and pulled the door open.

It was the Dreaditor.

Mum's dreaded editor, the terrible Nozomi Handa: shiny black hair in a sharp bob with a fringe, flashing dark eyes, red lips and, today, a tight dress of black and white zigzags. The woman who could make Mum crumple with a single flick of her blue pencil. The woman who had sent Mum a list of editorial 'suggestions' on the first three chapters of *Mermaid Girls 3* that was longer than the chapters. She was, quite definitely, not a birthday present.

'Um. Sorry,' mumbled Pea, stepping back and looking miserably at Mum. 'It's for you.'

But Mum was striding towards them with a beaming smile of welcome. She and the Dreaditor exchanged air kisses on the doorstep; then Mum pressed Pea forward with a firm hand on her back. The Dreaditor bent down, and Pea received her own air kisses, one for each cheek, but without touching.

'Happy birthday, Bree, darling, and you too, you funny little thing,' said the Dreaditor, giving Pea an awkward pat. 'I'm so thrilled to be here. Now, wherever shall we put this?'

The Dreaditor reached out with a pointed toe, and tapped her shiny shoe against a cardboard box that was resting on the doorstep.

'Well, since it's for Pea, I suppose she'd better carry it in,' said Mum, exchanging a most unusual grin with the Dreaditor.

Pea did as she was told. The box was wide, flattish, and quite heavy. It wasn't wrapped in shiny paper, though; it was ordinary brown cardboard.

'Is that really her present?' said Tinkerbell, wrinkling her nose.

'Part of it,' said Mum. 'Do come in, Nozomi. Say hello, girls!'

Clover and Tinkerbell survived more air kisses (Clover had been watching closely and enacted hers with perfect grace; Tinkerbell was less keen, and walked backwards as the Dreaditor advanced – until they ended up in the kitchen, where they politely shook hands instead). Pea stood there holding her box, entirely bewildered.

They sat in the front room, Pea on the floor with her cardboard box, the others all sitting and watching. It felt quite strange to have the

Dreaditor there in her zigzag frock and her spiky shoes.

'Now,' said Mum, 'you might have been wondering why I suddenly had to lock up my study.'

Pea sighed. 'I know why. It's your new book. You aren't doing any more mermaids. You're doing books for grown-up people, about house prices and kissing and nuclear war.'

'Are you?' said Clover, looking shocked.

'Really?' said Tinkerbell.

'No!' said Mum. 'Wherever did you get that idea?'

'Your interview!' said Pea. 'You told that journalist that now your children were growing up you couldn't keep writing about mermaids. And then you locked the study, and you didn't want us to see your new book, so I knew it must be about adult things. You haven't mentioned Lorelei or Coraly or Shelley for ages, or asked me to help with ideas. And now the Drea— Nozomi's here

266

to talk about your new book, even though it's my birthday.'

Mum and Nozomi laughed and laughed. Mum laughed so hard she made little hooting noises, like a happy owl – until Tinkerbell tugged her sleeve, and she saw Pea's face. She stopped at once, leaned forward and said, very seriously, 'Sweetheart, I haven't mentioned *my* new book because I've been busy with . . . Well, open the box.'

Pea peeled back the sticky tape and opened the flaps. On top was some scrunched-up paper. Underneath were books. Rainbow-coloured, and glossy; twelve of them, in two neat piles.

Pea's Book was the title.

Where the author's name usually went, it said Pea Llewellyn.

Clover and Tinkerbell both gasped out loud, but Pea was too stunned to make a sound. She picked one of them up, sliding her finger across the curly writing where her name was. Her name, on a book, as she'd always dreamed. There was even a drawing of Sky, the girl who lived on the moon. Inside, on the first page, it said:

For my brilliant daughter Pea, on her birthday
With all my love, Mum

The next page was a list of stories:

Contents

1: A Girl Called Sky

2: Sky, Moon-Dog, and the Mashed Potato Morning

3: Cloudier, the Girl from the Stars

4: Sky versus Space Ant (co-authored by Sam Paget-Skidelsky)

5: Sky versus the Space-Tigers of Jupiter (co-authored by Sam Paget-Skidelsky)

6: Amy James Goes Swimming

7: The Magical Hat

8: Mia Maloney, the Best Pirate of Them All

'You remember you lost your rainbow note-book?' said Mum. 'Well, I sort of lost it for you, so I could type up the stories. You nearly saw it on my desk one time, and then there were proofs to check before we got it printed – that why I locked up the study. I asked Nozomi whether she could help make it look more professional, and she suggested getting the illustrator of my books to make us a cover.'

'Oh, of course,' breathed Clover. 'I thought it looked familiar.'

It did too. Mum's *Mermaid Girls* covers had neat, flowy drawings of the characters, in beautiful sparkly-looking places. This one was different – the picture was smaller, and not of a mermaid, and the cover wasn't anywhere near as thick and shiny – but the whole thing had the same fluid look.

'Thank you,' whispered Pea shyly.

'Will it be in shops?' asked Tinkerbell.

'No – sorry, darling, even *I* can't make that happen,' said Mum. 'These are all the copies there are. We got them bound up by a printer Nozomi knows. Just enough for your book-launch party, so everyone has one to take home.'

'Book-launch party?' whispered Pea.

Mum nodded. 'Everyone's coming at twelve – the Paget-Skidelskys, and all your friends from school. And Clem, of course. Is that all right?'

Pea could barely breathe. She'd been to Mum's book launches before. Those were usually in book-shops, and Mum would wear her most mermaidy clothes, and complete strangers would come and tell her she was lovely.

'It's brilliant,' she whispered, hugging her book to her chest, while still reaching out to touch the rest, still in their box. 'Thank you thank you thank you.'

'And I thought I could offer an extra little some-thing, for "Marina Cove"'s writing daughter,' said the Dreaditor, her dark red lips curving. 'Shall we?'

Pea was taken to Mum's study for a fifteen-minute 'editorial meeting' with the Dreaditor. Mum came too – to make sure it was something nice to have on a birthday (the Dreaditor was dreaded for good reason). Once or twice Mum made a noisy little coughing sound; then the Dreaditor would catch her eye and break off at once from telling Pea that her endings needed to be more endingish, or that if her story was very short, not all of it should be descriptions of hair or explosions – and suddenly the talk would drift into asking Pea what she was reading, or if she enjoyed school.

But Pea didn't care. She loved it. She got to ask questions – about what sorts of stories the Dreaditor most liked to read (histories were her favourite, apparently – Pea resolved to rewrite her abandoned *Diary of Anne Boleyn* at once), and if any twelve-year-olds had ever had their books published properly, to go in shops, by Marchpane Books (which was a no, but one seventeen-year-old had, which the Dreaditor said was not long to wait).

Pea's book-launch party was even more wonderful.

Clem arrived early, overflowing with hugs and clutching more presents – though he said that none of his could possibly be as good as *Pea's Book*.

Mum had sent sneaky 'Mystery Party' invitations to all Pea's friends, so they couldn't give the game away. Bethany arrived quite convinced that 1-Click Dream were going to be there to perform a private concert, and had painted I ♥ 1-CD on her cheeks (backwards, unfortunately; it had looked the right way round in the mirror). Molly had her swimming costume on under her clothes, in case it turned out to be a swimming party. But Shruti, Eloise, and Reema from the Kensal Rise Kites all came in partyish outfits, and the Paget-Skidelskys were just in normal coming-round-on-a-Saturday clothes.

In any case, once they saw the pile of books on the coffee table, and Pea sitting behind them, glowing with pride, no one cared at all.

'Wow,' said Sam One when he saw his name inside. 'Double, triple, quadruple wow.'

'This is way better than a sleepover,' said Molly.

'Or a Hawaiian Dream,' said Eloise.

'If it was my party I'd rather have a special private concert,' said Bethany, 'but I suppose for you this is kind of the same thing.'

Pea thought it was better. Mum did an 'introduction', and then the Dreaditor did another one, telling them all what a brilliant book it was, and how only people who were there would ever have one of these special books. Surprise almost ruined the moment by leaping onto the table, snatching up a book in his mouth, and disappearing up the stairs with it, pursued by howls of, 'Drop it! No biting! Ow!' from Sam Two. But Sam One said that could be his copy, as one with bite marks wouldn't get mixed up with anyone else's.

Mum got Pea to read a few paragraphs of *A Girl Called Sky*. It made her blush fiercely, and she kept stopping to say, 'I'm sorry, I wrote this ages ago, I'd do it better now,' and 'This bit's silly – sorry,' until Dr Skidelsky shouted, 'Cobblers! Just read it!' and made everyone laugh. After that it was a bit easier. She even enjoyed it, a tiny bit, and everyone clapped.

'Cake and nibbly bits in the kitchen, everyone!' said Mum.

The cake was a squidgy chocolate square with twelve candles, arranged in the shape of a smiling face. There was still half of Mum's face cake too, which everyone admired. Pea ate three mini sausage rolls, and blew out her candles. Then they relit them so Mum could blow them out too.

Tinkerbell put on her chewed top hat, and showed off her Wuffly doggy choc trick for everyone.

Pea left them all watching it in the front room, and went to have a quiet moment in the study.

'Everything all right, birthday twin?' said Mum, peeping round the door.

'Better than all right,' said Pea, gazing at her book cover. 'Although . . . what *is* your new book about?'

Mum grinned, and disappeared for a moment. When she came back, she was holding a big envelope.

'Nozomi didn't only bring you a birthday present today,' she said. 'And – oh, you did guess one thing right. There won't be any more *Mermaid Girls* books.'

Pea clutched her book even more tightly.

'Oh, don't look so worried! I think you might like this even better. You know in the last book, there was the Dread Pirate Ellis, and the ghost ship at the end? Well . . . this is only a rough, remember – the finished thing will be much more shiny.'

She slid a sheet of paper out of the envelope.

It was a book cover, with a tall ship on a sparkly sea. *Pirate Girls*, it said across the top, with a skull and crossbones in the dot of each 'i'. On the ship were two girls with eye-patches and swords.

275

Behind them floated a ghostly mermaid with flowing red hair.

'Is that – Coraly?' whispered Pea.

Mum nodded. 'I couldn't bear to say goodbye to my mermaids for ever, so they'll still pop up every now and then.'

'And you aren't secretly writing a boring grown-up book with a shoe on the cover as well?'

'No!'

'Will *Pirate Girls* still be by Marina Cove?'

'Of course!'

'Why didn't you tell us?'

'I had to find out if Nozomi liked the idea first. And then, well, I've been a bit busy with someone else's book.'

They both grinned.

There was a gentle tap at the door.

'Can you sign my book, please, Pea?' asked Molly, holding her copy open on the first page.

Pea bit her lip. She had dreamed of this moment

for so long – and now, here it was, happening at her mum's desk, on her birthday. The other guests began lining up behind Molly, waiting to have theirs signed too.

She'd practised Mum's signature a million times, the loopy weird sort that no one could read. She hadn't worked out one of those for herself yet, though, so she settled for writing it fairly sensibly, in case she did something complicated and couldn't make it look the same a second time.

> To Molly,
> Thank you for coming to my birthday party
> and I hope you like my book.
> From Pea xx

In Mum's books, after Marina Cove's message, Pea had always drawn a leaping fish. But this was a book by Pea Llewellyn, so she thought it ought to have something else instead. She hesitated, trying to think what might fit her best.

She drew a smiling face: two quick strokes for eyes and a big smile.

ʊ‿ʊ

'I love it,' said Mum, peeking over her shoulder.

'Me too,' said Pea.

Dear Evan Magruder,

It is my birthday today! It's a shame you didn't come to my party, but I had the best present I could ever possibly have, so it turns out it doesn't matter.

After my book-launch party we went to the theatre and watched Clover being Alice in Wonderland/a grey slug. Mostly Clover pretended to be asleep, but the beginning and end where she was being awake were very brilliant – only Mum says we shouldn't say so too often as she already has a big head. (She doesn't; it's the same size as always – especially with the flatter hair – but she did refuse to

do the hoovering before my party because
'Actors don't hoove', which isn't even true.)

Tinkerbell has decided to become the
Amazing Tinkerbell and Her Magical Dogs when
she grows up. Dr Skidelsky says 'magical'
is not the word she would use to describe
Surprise but if Tinkerbell can make the smell of
wee disappear from carpet she will go far.

Mum says she'll need lots of my help with
the first Pirate Girls story, and she might call
one Mia after the pirate in my book.

This is a Better Letter so I won't actually
be sending it anyway, but I wanted to let you
know that I will not be writing you any more
letters. It turns out I don't need you, after
all. And I have a new book to write, which will
keep me very busy.

Love from Pea xx

SUSIE DAY

The Secrets of Billie Bright
9780141375335

The Secrets of Sam and Sam
9780141375281

Pea's Book of Best Friends
9780141375328

Pea's Book of Big Dreams
9780141375311

Pea's Book of Birthdays
9780141375298

Pea's Book of Holidays
9780141375304

Warning! These books do not contain mermaids.